Copyright © 2012
ISBN 978-0-9907043-4-8

**

"Congratulations on completing the book! I can't wait to read it as I edit -- and quite frankly you are among the finest writers I work with."
~Scott Philip Stewart, Ph.D. Christian Author

Introduction

Suspend disbelief and enter the world of angels. What is heaven like? What do angels do?

Venture back to "Before the Beginning" and watch what happens when mankind is added to the equation.

Join the hosts of angels as Heaven comes alive with plots, intrigue, and rebellion, all of which are invisible to the world of man.

The Laws of Heaven and Earth override the events of men and angels. They are the foundations upon which the heavens were founded. As with all laws, there are dire consequences for breaking these laws – and Satán believes that God has broken his own laws.

Disclaimer

One Angel's Opinion is not scripture. It is fiction, although, it illustrates scriptural truths.

The purpose of this book is to encourage people to trust God, even if they have unanswered questions.

At the back are answers to questions the reader may have concerning scriptural aspects of this book.

Acknowledgements:

My heartfelt thanks go to my husband Lee and my daughter Christina for their love, understanding, editing, and support.

To my friend Donalee Darby who read the manuscript, encouraged, and added her ideas and thoughts.

To my friend Carl Anderson, who read the manuscript and added his deep and scholarly insights.

To my assistant Lillian Grimes for her persistent support.

Table of Contents

Reference Sheet: A Cast of Characters _____ *pg* vi
Reference Sheet: A Division of God's Heavens _____ *pg* vii
Reference Sheet: The Underworld _____ *pg* viii
Reference Sheet: A Map of the Third Heaven _____ *pg* ix
Reference Sheet: A Map of Everything _____ *pg* x

Chapter One: Before the Beginning _____ *pg* 1
Chapter Two: Anticipation _____ *pg* 2
Chapter Three: Creation: _____ *pg* 3
Chapter Four: The Vault _____ *pg* 6
Chapter Five: Lucifer's Fall _____ *pg* 10
Chapter Six: Summoned _____ *pg* 12
Chapter Seven: An Assignment for Twins _____ *pg* 14
Chapter Eight: Etán _____ *pg* 16
Chapter Nine: Entrance _____ *pg* 17
Chapter Ten: Preparations _____ *pg* 18
Chapter Eleven: Araboth _____ *pg* 20
Chapter Twelve: Lucifer's Assignment _____ *pg* 21
Chapter Thirteen: Foreboding _____ *pg* 22
Chapter Fourteen: Big Plans _____ *pg* 23
Chapter Fifteen: Take Off _____ *pg* 25
Chapter Sixteen: The Fall of Man _____ *pg* 26
Chapter Seventeen: A Quake _____ *pg* 28
Chapter Eighteen: No Other Rock _____ *pg* 29
Chapter Nineteen: Consequences _____ *pg* 30
Chapter Twenty: Kasdaye and Marcus _____ *pg* 31
Chapter Twenty One: The Cavern of Hades _____ *pg* 33
Chapter Twenty Two: God's Perspective _____ *pg* 34
Chapter Twenty Three: Rumors _____ *pg* 35
Chapter Twenty Four: Civil War! _____ *pg* 37
Chapter Twenty Five: The Secret Things _____ *pg* 39
Chapter Twenty Six: Opius Kele Ursala Lynx _____ *pg* 42
Chapter Twenty Seven: Recruiting _____ *pg* 44
Chapter Twenty Eight: A Different Garden _____ *pg* 45
Chapter Twenty Nine: Nothing Like This _____ *pg* 47
Chapter Thirty: The Candidate _____ *pg* 48
Chapter Thirty One: It Is True _____ *pg.* 51
Chapter Thirty Two: Brothers _____ *pg* 53
Chapter Thirty Three: Ideas _____ *pg* 54
Chapter Thirty Four: Adam's Gardener _____ *pg* 55
Chapter Thirty Five: Adam's Greatest Fear _____ *pg* 56
Chapter Thirty Six: Talk Business _____ *pg* 59
Chapter Thirty Seven: A Tarnished Crown _____ *pg* 60

Table of Contents (continued)

Chapter Thirty Eight: A Needed Rest — pg 63
Chapter Thirty Nine: The Hierarchy — pg 64
Chapter Forty: East of Eden — pg 66
Chapter Forty One: Marcus — pg 67
Chapter Forty Two: Nod — pg 68
Chapter Forty Three: The Attic — pg 69
Chapter Forty Four: Tables Turned — pg 70
Chapter Forty Five: The Pit — pg 70
Chapter Forty Six: A Different Substitute — pg 72
Chapter Forty Seven: Not His Keeper — pg 74
Chapter Forty Eight: Perseus and Pyro — pg 74
Chapter Forty Nine: Cain's Birthright — pg 75
Chapter Fifty: The Daughter of a Man — pg 76
Chapter Fifty One: Confusion — pg 78
Chapter Fifty Two: A Lone Rebel — pg 79
Chapter Fifty Three: Transplant — pg 82
Chapter Fifty Four: Provision — pg 84
Chapter Fifty Five: Desolation — pg 85
Chapter Fifty Six: Relieved — pg 86
Chapter Fifty Seven: Frogs — pg 87
Chapter Fifty Eight: Satán's Shame — pg 88
Chapter Fifty Nine: Teardrop — pg 90
Chapter Sixty: Finding Eve's Descendent — pg 91
Chapter Sixty One: Enoch — pg 92
Chapter Sixty Two: Seven Golden Arches — pg 93
Chapter Sixty Three: Signs of Wrath — pg 95
Chapter Sixty Four: Seventy Times Seven — pg 96
Chapter Sixty Five: An Offer — pg 97
Chapter Sixty Six: Promoting Evil — pg 99
Chapter Sixty Seven: It Happened — pg 102
Chapter Sixty Eight: Without Excuse — pg 103
Chapter Sixty Nine: Memories — pg 105
Chapter Seventy: A Proper Order — pg 108
Chapter Seventy One: Rest - Comfort — pg 109
Chapter Seventy Two: Captured — pg 111
Chapter Seventy Three: Patience — pg 112
Chapter Seventy Four: A Dove — pg 112
Chapter Seventy Five: Surprised — pg 113
Chapter Seventy Six: Catching Up — pg 115

Questions about One Angel's Opinion and Scriptural Truths — pg 121

An Alphabetical Cast of Characters Reference Sheet

1. **Acamar/Akkamar:** A fallen angel, second in command to Lucifer/Satán in Satán's hierarchy. He is the Angel of Chaos.
2. **Aqua:** The angel of water. He is an elemental angel.
3. **Auroran:** The scribe who authors this book. He is the studious twin of Borealis and the keeper of the keys.
4. **Borealis:** The adventurous twin of Auroran. When he is advanced to Bene-angel he is free to choose his own assignments.
5. **Choices**: An Offering Angel. Choices carries a scale to weigh values while roaming the earth with the angel Wisdom.
6. **Chronos**: A scribe who reports to Auroran as a "chronicler."
7. **D'shubba:** Overseer of *the Honorarium*, Heaven's library of learning. He is like a monk full of wisdom and grace.
8. **Etán:** A hulk-like fallen angel in Satán's hierarchy. He is the angel of war and violence.
9. **Gabriel:** Replaces Lucifer as the administrator of the heavens.
10. **Jo'el**: A tinker angel who studies the souls of men, documenting his research.
11. **Kairos:** A scribe who reports to Auroran and who is able to discern divine moments in the events of men.
12. **Kasdaye:** A fallen angel in Satán's hierarchy. He is the angel of demonic practices.
13. **Lucifer aka Satán:** The Archangel who rebelled and becomes *Ha* (the) *Satán* (adversary/accuser) of men, aka: the devil. He is synonymous with the reptilian "snake/dragon/Leviathan." He is the angel of deception, betrayal and lies.
14. **Lyrid Mot:** A fallen angel in Satán's hierarchy. He is the angel of sickness, disease, and misery.
15. **Marcus:** A fallen angel in Satán's hierarchy. He is the handsome angel of self pleasures and addictions.
16. **Menkib:** A warrior angel and Zuben's side-kick.
17. **Michael:** The secluded angel, ready to be revealed at the calling out of the Chosen Ones. He is the protective angel of the Hebrews.
18. **OKUL:** A Tinker angel who works in the Honorarium, answering questions and giving insight to the angels.
19. **Pene-muel:** A scribe for Satán. A fallen angel but not one of Satán's hierarchy; but rather, one of Satán's "mules."

20. **Perseus:** A warrior angel who becomes smitten by Zillah, a daughter of men.

21. **Pyro**: The angel of fire. He is an elemental angel.
22. **Tyl:** A temple angel.
23. **Wisdom:** An Offering Angel. Gives everything on earth a spiritual value. He works in tandem with Choices.
24. **Zuben:** A warrior angel known for his loyalty and remarks of humor. He is also called a "strong" angel.

The Divisions of God's Heavens
A Reference Sheet

The Third Heaven

> "I know a man in Christ who fourteen years ago—whether in the body I do not know, or whether out of the body I do not know, God knows—such a one was caught up to the third heaven." 2 Cor 12:2

I. **Ma'on** The City of God – in the third Heaven. "Yet He had commanded the clouds (of angels) above, And opened the doors of heaven" (Psalm 78:23).

II. **Zebul** Where the Temple of God overlooks the kingdom and the City of God (Ma'on) in the third Heaven. "The LORD is in His holy temple, The LORD's throne is in heaven; His eyes behold, His eyelids test the sons of men" (Psalm 11:4).

III. **Wilon** The forest of the third Heaven.

IV. **Raki'a** Where The arches of Heaven form a confluence.

V. **Makon** The storehouses of God. "The Lord cast down large hailstones from heaven on them as far as Azekah, and they died." (Joshua 10:11)

VI. **Shehaqim** An outpost of Heaven in Paradise.

The Seventh Heaven
The Heaven of Heavens

VII. **Araboth**, the Throne Room of God. He sits in clouds of darkness above the third Heaven.

> "But will God indeed dwell on the earth? Behold, heaven and the heaven of heavens cannot contain You. How much less this temple which I have built! (1 Kings 8:27)

> "The LORD has established His throne in Heaven, And His kingdom rules over all" (Psalm 103:19).

> He bowed the heavens also, and came down: and darkness was under his feet. (Psalm 18:9)

> O Lord, our Lord, how excellent is thy name in all the earth! who hast set thy glory above the heavens. (Psalm 8:1)

The Underworld

The Bottomless Pit:
[*Woe to the Wicked*] "Indeed, because he transgresses by wine, He is a proud man, and he does not stay at home. Because he enlarges his desire as hell, and he *is* like death, and cannot be satisfied, He gathers to himself all nations and heaps up for himself all peoples" (Habakkuk 2:5).

"And they had as king over them, the angel of the bottomless pit, whose name in Hebrew is Abaddon, but in Greek he has the name Apollyon" (Revelation 9:11).

Sheol
Sheol is the place of the dead. It holds the dislodged souls from the River of the Living and includes both Paradise and Hades. "Let us swallow them alive like Sheol, and whole, like those who go down to the Pit" (Proverbs 1:12).

Paradise
Paradise is one area of Sheol. Paradise includes an area known as Abraham's bosom. The place where believing souls, who have died go to wait for their Redeemer. "So it was that the beggar died, and was carried by the angels to Abraham's bosom. The rich man also died and was buried. And being in torments in Hades, he lifted up his eyes and saw Abraham afar off, and Lazarus in his bosom" (Luke 16:22-23)

Hades
Hades is another area of Sheol. Hades is the place where non-believing souls go after they have died. Satán's cavern is also there. "So it was that the beggar died, and was carried by the angels to Abraham's bosom. The rich man also died and was buried. And being in torments in Hades, he lifted up his eyes and saw Abraham afar off, and Lazarus in his bosom" (Luke 16:22-23).

The River of the Living
The River of the Living separates Paradise from Hades. It holds the souls of all living men which float like bubbles upon the river. It runs at the bottom of a deep chasm separating Paradise and Hades. No one is able to cross this river. When souls die they are dislodged from the river. A light soul floats to Paradise while a heavy soul is caught in the mire and mud on the beaches of Hades.

A Map of the Heavens
A Reference Sheet
(Araboth is the seventh heaven above the other heavens)

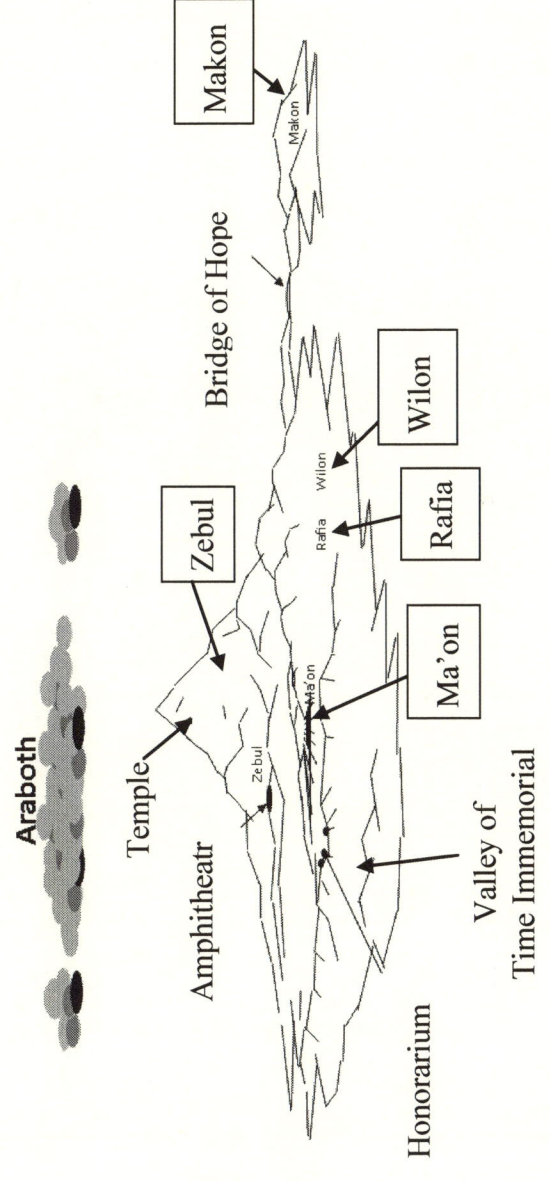

A MAP OF EVERYTHING – *A Reference Sheet*

Araboth (outside the bubble) is the seventh heaven. It encapsulates all creation including the third heaven. Like a mother's womb, God carries and protects his creation. The Bottomless pit is a shaft (a hole) piercing the heavens and the universe running the entirety of North to South. It is indeed bottomless.

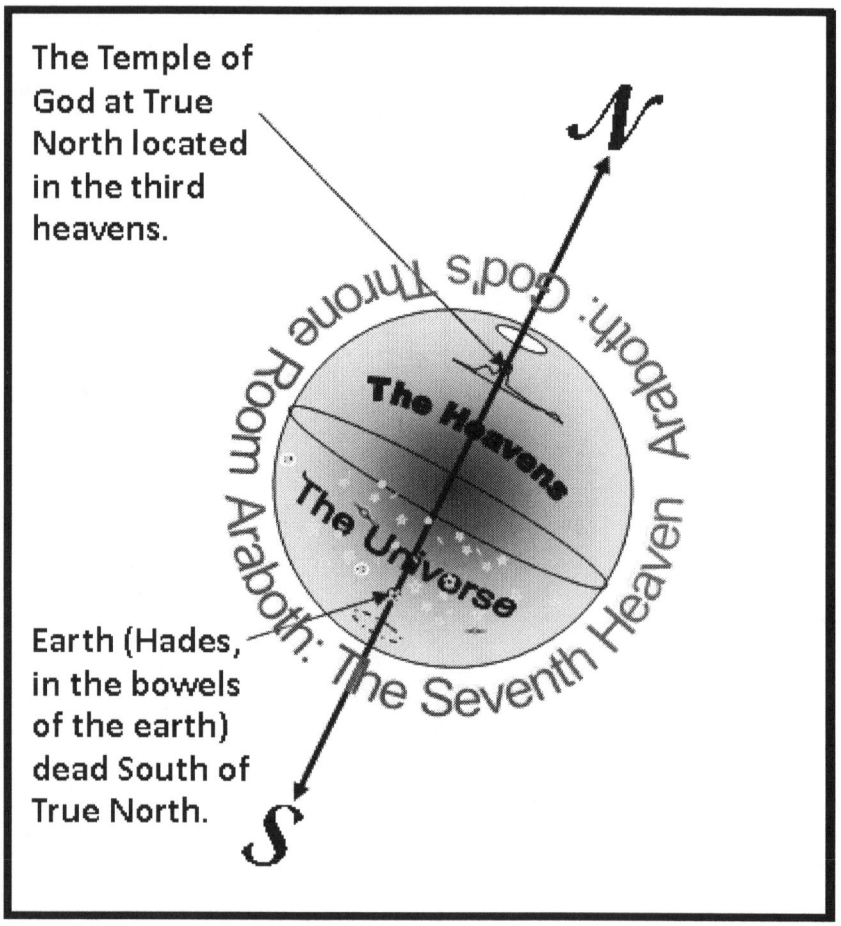

The Bottomless Pit intersects both Hades in the bowels of the earth, and God's temple, located at True North in the heavens. The bottomless pit in Hades is "dead" south of the bottomless pit in God's temple at True North.

It is a place of refuse, of unclean things. It is also called hell. It has a king called The Destroyer who destroys anything that is unclean.

Before the Beginning
Chapter One

Auroran's robe swept the marble floors as he hustled through the Honorarium and turned left into Emet Kadosh, the library of Holy Truth. He was on a mission. His keys, dangling on his hip, jangled as he walked. Upon entering Emet Kadosh he went straight to the back of the room, to a cabinet framed with transparent panes of electrified energy where he found what he was looking for.

When he unlocked the cabinet, the humming panes of energy ceased. He reached in and pulled a book gently from its shelf. He ran his finger up and down the spine, feeling the engraved title in the binding: *The Events of Men and Angels.*

He thought back to before the beginning of mankind where the story began - so long ago; back when he couldn't have understood the implications of mankind's creation on the future of the angels. Auroran sighed deeply. *Now he finally understood that which he, himself, had documented so long ago.* Eager to read the book anew, he took his seat and felt himself relax as his eyes began the lazy read, scanning the first words written:

"In the days of old, before the beginning, God met in the holy of holies to make a Pact. This Pact was written by the Holy Spirit, for it is He who will engrave it upon the hearts of men. It was signed in blood by the Son of God, destined to become the Lamb slain from the foundation of the world, and authorized by the Father, the divine Judge who upholds the Laws and Ordinances of Heaven. This Pact became God's covenant with man whom He had not yet created.

The Son of God spoke saying, 'With a song of thanksgiving I will sacrifice myself. What I have vowed I will make good.'

Thunder and Lightning shook the heavens as the Father and the Spirit witnessed the Son of God morph into a Lamb. Lightning struck the Lamb splitting it violently in half, covering it in blood and laid out. The Father and the Spirit walked between the pieces of the splayed Lamb to seal the Pact all had agreed to – a covenant of death never to be broken.

The blood of the Lamb ran down into a gully, pooling up and hardening, forming a cornerstone upon which the laws and ordinances of heaven will be laid; those stones of fire to become the foundations of the heavens and the earth.

The Pact was then sealed with seven seals, such that none of God's creatures could open it; not even Lucifer, who came to walk among the stones of fire."

Auroran stopped his reading to pause and think about the irony of this book he wrote, because it was more than the history of the events of men and angels but his own history as well. Then he eagerly read on . . .

"The angel Auroran, a scribe in God's service, chosen by God, sent invitations to all creatures in God's realm, requesting the honor of their presence to a most auspicious event – a new creation."

Anticipation
Chapter Two

The anticipation of this event became the centerpiece of conversations throughout the heavenly realms of the eleventh dimension. Heady with excitement, angels pondered its significance until the propitious day arrived. As angels began to arrive, the amphitheater twinkled with the arrival of hosts making their way to the mount of the congregation. Angels came from afar, each one a point of light drawing nearer and nearer, folding and unfolding through myriads of spiritual dimensions, eager to arrive at their destination.

Warrior angels came arrayed in formal military attire with epaulets on their shoulders and sashes across their chests. The temple angels wore robes of linen representing righteousness, attendants had garlands about their heads, and messengers wore sashes wrapped around their chests. Scribes and administrators arrived in heavy robes while service angels donned braided belts and tassels. They came in full regalia – crowns, sashes, cummerbunds, medallions, and capes; for it would have been inappropriate for one *not* to display their hard earned status at such an assembly as this.

Auroran darted back and forth verifying each invitation as the guests arrived. The amphitheater sparkled like the dust of diamonds on the paved stones of glory. Each angel shone with the Glory of God.

After the last angel arrived, Auroran took his assigned seat alongside his twin brother, Borealis. The two angels overheard other angels speculating among themselves as to the meaning of this rare and unequaled event. Auroran leaned into his brother to whisper his own thoughts. The two shared their opinions on how this creation might look, how it would affect the work of the angels, and what their respective roles might be. Two other angels, Wisdom and Choices, sat on the other side of Borealis. They had special invitations, indicating perhaps - they were to play a special role in this creation.

Expectations heightened. The amphitheater teemed with angels abuzz in conversation. Then, as darkness settled over the theatre, a hush ensued. The stars of God brightened against the emerging darkness. Auroran and Borealis looked around to see what had caused this change in energy. Faces turned as the brilliant necklace of all created beings, Lucifer himself, the archangel of archangels, administrator in the affairs of Heaven, entered. The train of his long robe flowed in the wake of his presence. Beauty, passion, and fire emanated from his flawless being as his long yellow hair glistened around his face. With each movement Lucifer reflected the majestic light of God's glory, dazzling all who were in his presence.

Auroran noted how Lucifer, upon reaching his high seat of authority in the arena's balcony, turned and scanned the audience. With a wide sweep of his hand, he signaled for silence before taking his seat. The amphitheater became as silent as the night sky. Each angel knew something great was about to happen.

Creation
Chapter Three

Slowly, the tapestries of creation opened.

An explosion of Light revealed the very presence of the Almighty, the source of all energy, light, and life.

Angels fell to their faces to bow low to Him who is from everlasting to everlasting. As the angels rose, they lifted their hands toward His glory shouting, "Blessing and honor and glory and power to Him who sits on the throne." Others joined, shouting, "Holy, holy, holy is the Lord God Almighty!"

A veil dropped to separate the intensity of God's glory from the angels. For many, this was their first encounter with the presence of the Almighty. They were now able to watch as He began his work of old.

The angels Wisdom and Choices were called upon for assistance.

- - - - -

In a moment of time, a bejeweled fireworks display burst forth with a majestic panorama of vivid colors never before seen, exploding in new and glorious dimensions and casting forth galaxies, star clusters, nebulas, and black holes.

Angels stared in wonderment as comets raced through the heavens, nebulas exploded, suns radiated, and moons reflected light from afar. Ever so gradually, the dance of creation slowed against the soft operatic music of the heavens. Like ballet dancers, illustrious skirts of the galaxies pirouetted ever so softly across the background of the heavens as the Spirit of God moved across the face of the waters of the deep. Like the gentle fingers of a harpist, the Spirit created ripples of harmonic movement.

The foundations of the universe were established according to the laws and ordinances of God's own character.

Day by day God separated the light from the darkness, the heights from the depths, the depths from the breadths, and the ether from the matter. After forming the earth, God set it on the edge of man's galaxy so that man, yet to be created, would have a window into his own universe. God also made the sun's diameter 400 times the moon's diameter and set the sun exactly 400 times farther away from the earth so man would be able to experience eclipses enabling him to see deeply into the heavens. The eclipse was God's signature thumbprint on His creation.

Next, God separated the waters above the earth from the waters below the earth. Water crystallized drop by drop around the orb of the earth creating a canopy of ice. This special planet soon teemed with trees, grasses, shrubs, ferns, and flowers. Creature after creature appeared each one after its kind.

All the angels, the morning stars, and the sons of God sang for joy at God's workmanship!

The voice of the Triune God rumbled through the heavens as The Father, The Son, and The Holy Spirit declared one to another "Let us make man in the Image of our own glory, according to our Likeness, and let them rule over the fish of the sea and the birds of the air and over the beasts of the field and over the whole earth."

The angels leaned in to watch God create a being called "man."

From the dust of the ground, from the physical matter of the universe, God pulled forth strands of DNA, twisting them around and around, until man's physical make-up appeared on the canvas of Heaven.

Man was perfect in every way, from his eternal body to his eternal soul. God saw to it the cells in his body continually regenerated, making him an eternal masterpiece. God called him "Adam" because he was the first man and he was made from the ground.

God was entirely satisfied with his work and declared it to be good – filled with perfection, completeness, and satisfaction. God gave dominion over the earth and everything in it, to Adam.

Lucifer, who had been watching the creation in earnest, suddenly snapped his head forward to hear more. *What? What had God said? Did he say this "man" would rule over the whole earth?* His senses immediately heightened. He felt as though something was amiss as he watched God breathe His life-giving breath into the man, creating a soul that consisted of a conscience, emotions, thoughts, and free will. Man's physical body existed in the first four dimensions, but man's soul resided in the eleventh dimension, in the spirit world of the angels.

Furthermore, God created man with a strange thirteenth dimension, the dimension of dreams. Man's dreams gave man the ability to communicate and connect with God in a way angels could not.

The angels drew their breath in amazement; thirteen was the holiest number associated with God's name and His unity. Unification with God meant a unified heart in belief and devotion.

Lucifer shivered as unnerving thoughts stirred within his being. *Not a single angel in Heaven had this kind of access to God. What is man that God has set His heart on him?* Lucifer bristled as he debated within himself. *Was not he, Lucifer, the only angel appointed to oversee all God's creations? Why then would man have dominion over the earth and not he? How unsettling God had not disclosed all of this to him; after all, he was Heaven's highest archangel, the administrator of the affairs of Heaven.* Lucifer squirmed, thinking: *Surely God will soon put my concerns to rest.*

Lucifer forced himself to focus on God's activities. God was now in the process of creating a mate for Adam.

By manipulating the DNA in Adam's rib, God created a woman and named her "Eve." She would be the mother of all mankind. When the man woke and discovered the woman, he loved her. Upon touching, their souls merged and clung one to the other, two opalescent bubbles sharing one membrane, they became as one. The angels pondered this concept. Within these two souls resided emotions as deep as the universe itself, with creative thoughts and a will for choices.

Lucifer marveled at God's handiwork. *The man and woman are indeed a work of art! The passion they share is admirable.* However; he immediately identified the fact that the woman was man's weakness. Lucifer reveled in the fact he himself was immune to such feelings. Admirable or not, this crown of creation still left him unsettled.

Angelic applause filled the heavens as the rich, heavy tapestries of creation slowly drew to a close. It had been a perfect six days.

On the seventh day, God rested from all His work. God blessed the seventh day and made it holy.

Behind the veil, unbeknownst to the angelic host, God smiled at His handiwork. The universe had been wound like a clock with every star set in its place such that right on time and according to His own foreknowledge, signs and wonders would appear in the sky for all men to behold and to signify supernatural events.

The Vault
Chapter Four

As the angels left the amphitheater, Borealis said to Auroran, "I cannot comprehend this universe. Is it infinitely large? Does it have an edge?"

Auroran, known among the angels as the studious angel, answered: "Unlike us, mankind does not have the ability to travel faster than light. Even at the speed of light it would take him 100,000 man-years to traverse the diameter of just his own galaxy, and his galaxy is but one of billions and billions."

"Then it would be *impossible* for man to travel across his *own* galaxy, let alone into another galaxy." exclaimed Borealis, exuberant.

"Do remember, however," Auroran reminded him, "men are eternal creatures with far more than just 100,000 man-years to acquire the knowledge of travel."

Borealis wondered why God would create millions of galaxies in a tiny speck of night sky where it would appear from earth as though there were no stars at all. He pondered whether God created the stars so that man could populate the universe, or for no other purpose than man's enjoyment in watching the night sky.

"Space and time are strange things," Auroran pointed out. "Look how God used time dilation to create this universe. Time expands with space. Fifteen billion years have passed in the universe since God began his creation, and the universe expanded a million-million times. If you divide 15 billion by a million-million you get .015 years or six man-days from earth's perspective, the ratio for time dilation."

Overhearing their conversation, the angel Pyro chimed in, "God made man to multiply. Some day, in some way, see if they do not fill the entire universe."

Pyro flamed when he was excited. Unlike other angels, he was able to emit flames from his being. He was known as the angel of fire.

Acamar, another angel, joined their conversation. "Auroran! You have the keys to the future. You can show us the future!"

After a thoughtful pause, Auroran agreed to take them to the vault in which God astutely kept the future locked away.

Just before they reached the vault, Pyro received an assignment and blinked out of sight. Angels never knew when they might be called upon for an assignment.

The remaining three, Auroran, Borealis, and Acamar turned aside; away from the throngs of angels leaving the auditorium. They made their way out of the arena and proceeded down a long, empty, ominous corridor. At the end of the hall, the steely vault room dominated the site.

Acamar hesitated, "Is this allowed?" Acamar felt uneasy. It was his nature. He hesitated whenever called upon to take the lead. God had created him to serve, but he desired more: He wanted to lead in spite of his nature. Often he felt invisible; this was one of those times. Perhaps he hadn't yet found his purpose. He thought back to the number of positions he tried, but even in music he didn't qualify. Perhaps he might have a special place in this new creation. Would he appear in mankind's future to play some key role? Everything was exciting – everything was uncertain.

As Acamar hesitated, Auroran and Borealis became preoccupied with new speculations, conversing back and forth.

Still buried in his thoughts, Acamar heard a noise, a hissing.

Pssssst. psssssst.

Acamar turned to find the strange noise. It came from a bush near the door. Behind the bush was a dark figure trying to get his attention, evidently without attracting the attention of Borealis and Auroran. The figure drew Acamar into his area and proceeded to sway him with provocative arguments. As they spoke Acamar heard Auroran finishing his conversation with his brother and unlocking the vaulted room. He left this dark figure in the shadows to rejoin Auroran and Borealis who never missed him.

"God entrusted me with the Eternal Ring of Keys, including the key to the future. I can't access everything, but I can allow this. . . ." Auroran pulled two keys from his sash (two was God's number of decision, and both keys were needed to unlock the box and reveal its proper contents). Auroran knew without both keys the future could turn up anything, but by using both keys simultaneously it showed the future God had decided upon – these two keys were called "Decided and Done."

Auroran alone among the angels knew it took both keys to see the proper future since it was one of the many secrets of God.

The three angels became mesmerized as they peered into the revealed future.

"See, this is how the earth will look in the ages to come." Auroran explained.

"Completely different," Acamar whispered.

"The ice canopy is missing!" Borealis pointed out. "And look, the earth is divided."

Acamar moved in closer. "I wonder how these changes will come to take place.... They are so drastic."

As Acamar pondered their revelations, Borealis blurted out, "I want to travel this universe!"

He announced it with such uninhibited eagerness Auroran began to laugh. *Borealis' adventurous spirit was so unlike his own.* Auroran was far more interested in studying God's plans for man than pursuing adventures. Auroran wondered *how could they be made from the same frequency of light and yet be so different.*

Auroran relocked the box, sealing the future off from undisciplined eyes forever.

The three companions left the vaulted area with Borealis and Auroran flanking Acamar. The threesome returned to the noisy, crowded arena leaving a trail of static as they picked their way through various cliques of angels. Moving in and out of diverse dimensions, they heard the crowds talking excitedly, tossing about speculations concerning this new creation.

Acamar wondered aloud if man might have been created to serve the angels. His speculations went unnoticed because Auroran and Borealis were distracted trying to find their way through the crowd.

"Look! Over there!" Borealis pointed out. "Lucifer is among us."

The three angels struggled to make their way toward the celebrated archangel. The static in the crowds caused each one of them to blink in and out of view erratically.

Just as they neared Lucifer, a messenger flew in and landed with news: "Did you hear? Did you hear?" he asked breathlessly.

"Hear what, my friend?" Auroran prodded.

"Michael's been promoted!" the angel replied. "He is now an archangel!"

Borealis raised one brow. "But there was no advancement assembly."

"I don't understand, either," the messenger beamed. "Nevertheless, Michael is now an archangel!" He flew off to deliver the news to others.

Lucifer, who was stationed close by, overheard the announcement. He found himself shaken to the very core of his being; once again he hadn't been apprised of this.

The placid waters of Lucifer's thoughts were disturbed, for God had not informed him of this promotion. Like an eddy, the disturbances first stirred then pulled foul questions from the floor of his suspicious heart to float upon the surface of his mind.

Auroran, Borealis, and Acamar joined the curious crowds who were inquiring as to the meaning of this mankind. They looked to Lucifer for answers. "What is your take on this, Lucifer?"

Lucifer composed himself before rising among them. "Like you, I confess I am equally surprised at the Creator's lack of forthcoming communication concerning this *mankind*. I promise to look into these matters and return with a report to help everyone understand more of this momentous occasion!" Lucifer raised his hands high in the air, smiling to his congregation.

An angel on the outer edge of the crowd shouted, "Do you have plans to enter the physical universe?"

Lucifer paused before answering. "Yes, that is my plan."

The crowd erupted in applause, but Auroran knew Lucifer should not be delving into this on his own. He drew in his breath. *You are playing with fire, Lucifer!*

Auroran noticed Lucifer pulling Acamar aside after the applause.

Borealis likewise spotted Lucifer speaking with Acamar. *This is a great honor for Acamar,* Borealis thought.

When Acamar returned he casually noted, "Lucifer asked me to do him a favor, but I am not allowed to discuss it."

"Ahh, a mystery," Auroran said.

Borealis, however, was crestfallen. He wanted more information than he was able to get.

"Did you feel that?" Auroran said, interrupting his friends.

"Feel what?" Borealis asked.

"A strange chill," Auroran said, trembling. "Something caused me to shudder." His friends were engrossed in their conversation, and so Auroran dismissed it. *A coming storm perhaps.*

Lucifer's Fall
Chapter Five

A plaster-faced, smiling Lucifer chose to slip away from the crowd. He wanted to be alone. He wandered back to the silent emptiness of the auditorium. There, in the middle of the arena, was a house-sized bubble set upon a floating ring of fire. Within the bubble, angels were able to watch man's activities on the earth. Thoughts raced through Lucifer's mind. *How much time would it take for him to reach this earth? If he entered this universe, would it be possible for angels to view his activities from this arena?*

Standing before the bubble, his motionless dark form stared not into the bubble but into the very abyss of his own thoughts where a bank of dark clouds had formed and were rumbling in potential rebellion.

Startled, Lucifer shuddered when Choices entered the auditorium. Lucifer quickly flashed a mask-like smile.

"I don't know why," Choices said, mystified, "but I felt you needed me."

Behind him, Wisdom also entered. "I felt called also."

The two angels marveled at such timing, sharing their experiences one with the other.

"Thank you, but no," Lucifer assured them. "I was just admiring this new creation."

"As am I," Choices replied.

"And I," Wisdom echoed.

When Lucifer returned to staring within the bubble, the two angels left the arena chatting, leaving Lucifer to himself.

Lucifer quickly revolved back to smoldering. He needed answers and he needed them immediately. *This,* he decided, *is the time for action!* He drew in a deep breath, stepped upon the ledge of fire and slipped his leg cautiously into the flexible, floating bubble. He felt a strange sensation ripple across his skin as his leg entered another space-time continuum. As he slipped his other leg into this strange new, bewildering expanse he shivered. Before he could catch his breath, the universe had sucked him in. He found himself in free fall, his hands reaching out, groping out in search of something, anything ... but there was nothing to grasp except dark, empty space. For the first time Lucifer felt cold, raw fear. It gripped his entire being. Headlong he hurled, head over heels, heels over head, not knowing up from down, not knowing how, where, or when it would end. He could not catch his breath. He gasped before he lost consciousness.

When he came to, some time later, he struggled to get himself upright without knowing where "up" might be. He fell through unknown dimensions restricted by laws of physics he did not understand. Strange forces had taken over. He was flung among the stars as a star, sliding through worm holes, stretched inside-out through a black hole, until finally his angelic body slowed to something manageable as he became acclimated to this strange new universe. He realized he had expanded his being into a parachute of sorts where he could soar through dimensions more hospitable to traveling this universe. His panic gave way to utter, desolate humiliation. Lost and alone, Lucifer the anti-hero made his way back to his heaven without having succeeded in finding man's earth. He asked himself, *Did anyone from the mount witness my humiliation?*

Summoned
Chapter Six

When Lucifer returned to the heavens at last, something had changed. It was as though his old reality had been replaced by another. Isolated and alone, he no longer felt as though he belonged in the heavens. He set about doing his administrative duties, saying nothing of his harrowing experience.

All around Lucifer the angels were busy with their assigned tasks, albeit enjoying opportunities to stop by the arena to look into the bubble and watch plants explode in abundance or listen in as Adam named the animals.

- - - - -

Auroran stopped by the arena to watch Eve play with a lamb who had taken a liking to her. It followed her throughout the Garden.

"Name this little lamb, Adam," she called to her husband as she sat on the lush grass cradling the gentle creature in her arms.

He looked at it, smiled, and called it *Seth*.

"Seth?" Eve laughed. "Why did you name it Seth?"

"Because," Adam answered, "if I can't see you but I can see the lamb, then I know you are nearby. It's like a substitute for you, since Seth means substitute."

The two laughed together as the lamb butted her shoulder, knocking her backwards.

Adam watched Eve. She seemed to draw him into her world. He loved the way she moved about the Garden so gracefully. He studied her neckline. *Why did the look in her eyes or the form of her body move him in such a way?* He listened to her sweet laughter echoing through the Garden.

Angels were mesmerized watching them.

Lucifer's countenance brightened when he realized the angels' attention had been so fixed on Adam and Eve that no one had seen his fall.

Eventually the routines of administration became the mainstay of angelic life. As before, everything continued as it had always been.

Lucifer stood in the hall of Legal Administration next to the Courts of Divine Justice listening to his assistant, Lyrid, when a messenger landed within their reach and announced he had been dispatched from the Judicial Court of the Divine Council.

"Hail, Lucifer! Greetings and salutations from the Throne Room of the Lord God Almighty. You are summoned to appear at the day, place, and time specified. Do you agree to do so?"

"I agree," Lucifer replied cautiously, his mouth slightly agape. He slowly accepted the summons, trying to hide the fact he was somewhat in shock. "Do you need my seal?"

"No," the messenger answered, "only your agreement, placed there."

A summons? What might this mean?

Dismissing the messenger, Lucifer opened his summons – slowly. Apprehension turned to exhilaration as he read the contents. *Finally,* Lucifer grinned, *God is taking me into His confidence!* He leaned over and exhaled gleefully.

His assistant watched him, amazed to see the Archangel of the heavens happy. "It must be good news," Lyrid surmised.

"Yes indeed, I believe it is." Lucifer slapped his solemn assistant on the back causing his small stature to stumble.

Lyrid raised his brows in surprise. Though small and spindly, Lyrid was loyal. *Things had certainly changed in the Heavens.*

With his spirit revitalized and his energy renewed, Lucifer was ready to return to his tasks. He immersed himself in his work with renewed fervor. On this bright day he left the hall of Legal Administration and walked to the Stones of Fire upon which the iron-clad finger of God had engraved all the laws of Heaven. Lucifer was adept at understanding the nuances of the laws and ordinances of Heaven. Upon these living Stones of Fire the foundations of the governments were laid –their fire inexhaustible, their words unalterable.

As he walked, he mentally reviewed his summons. He analyzed it and reanalyzed it. Then he found what he was looking for among the stones of fire– a tablet of protocol for this occasion.

Although it was customary for angels to receive orders directly from God via silent communication, often to blink out of sight, Lucifer could not recall a time when an angel had been summoned to God's own throne room. He had only heard rumors, what some called "myths," concerning Araboth from Tinker angels. In Araboth, God had set His throne high above the angels. It was said God's throne sat upon a canopy of darkness called "The fear of the LORD." *Lucifer did not believe he would feel this fear.*

An Assignment for Twins
Chapter Seven

Auroran was in the Honorarium, his place of work, perusing new editions of scrolls.

As he picked his way along, he noticed something new, unique in every way. With his interest piqued, he picked up a scroll to study it. He noticed it had been sealed with seven seals. *Seals are a sign of ownership. Only God Himself would seal a book with seven seals.* He eagerly turned to the title: *The Pact of the Triune God*. Auroran's immediate impulse was to look inside, but, woeful, he knew he had neither the authority nor the power to break the seals. In spite of his overwhelming curiosity, he was forced to return the scroll to its shelf. Oddly enough, he could see a Deed to the title of the earth had been inserted, its corners sticking out just far enough for Auroran to recognize it.

As Auroran studied the strange scroll, Borealis arrived to join him in a new assignment. Together, they were to make a map, a path of the stars in man's universe. They went to the arena and gazed into the bubble to gather the information. The angels had dubbed the bubble "Corona," for it seemed to be the very eye of God. Corona continually scanned the universe as well as events on the earth, stopping and focusing on those events of most interest to its viewers. Corona would fade out from earth to scan the universe or pull in to display the events of man.

Auroran had recruited Borealis in his endeavor to make a 3D model of this universe. Auroran's assignment was to make a map for angels such that they would be able to travel back and forth to earth to carry out God's assignments.

Auroran found pleasure in the map's accuracy, whereas Borealis saw it as a treasure map leading to unanticipated adventures.

The twins worked side by side: They measured the constellations and solar systems so they could draw them to scale when they depicted them in a hologram map-model. The pieces fit together in tiny chunks and sometimes a few tiny chunks fit together to become larger chunks.

Auroran smiled with unusual contentment. This, finally, was something he and his brother had in common, something they could work on together. Borealis' enthusiasm surprised Auroran, for Borealis was even more consumed in the project than he. But Auroran's countenance fell when Borealis suddenly stopped his work.

Borealis stood before Auroran with a chunk of the holographic universe dangling from his limp hand hanging at his side. He stared at Auroran.

Auroran froze, waiting for Borealis to speak.

"How long do you think this will take?" Borealis asked, hesitantly.

Auroran surveyed the pieces lying about. "An eternity?" He looked into Borealis' eyes and saw the complete restlessness.

"I cannot do this for an eternity," Borealis said, faltering.

Auroran saw his twin's desperate need to escape. "Yes, I see you cannot. This is my kind of work, Borealis. The focus and determination that drives me to passion will surely drive you to madness. Please, feel free to leave. You must find your own destiny."

"But, I don't want to abandon you," Borealis said, furrowing his brows.

"You already have, my brother," Auroran smiled. "Whether you are here physically, or gone, you are not here. This project will extend into the ages. Do you wish to wear that desperate look on your face throughout eternity?"

Borealis brightened. "Thank you for understanding. I want to be exploring this universe -not duplicating it. Perhaps I could bring back answers to our inexplicable questions." Borealis pointed out areas where he and Auroran had struggled.

"Go! Go, go ... *go*." Auroran patted his brother on the back with one hand and pushed him on his way with the other.

Borealis could not hide his relief. He flew off into a future he was eager to explore.

Etán
Chapter Eight

The Mountain of God filled the landscape of the eye in Zebul. Just below the peak, located at Truth North sat the Temple of God. At the base of the mountain, an Amphitheatre filled the hollowed embrasure of a smaller mountain. As the landscape tapered off the Forest of God thinned out into the beautifully landscaped Raki'a and Wilon where the Arches of God were known for their breathtaking beauty. On the flatland, in Ma'on, the Honorarium, the hall of Legal Administration, the Courts of Divine Justice, and the Assembly Hall lined the streets paved with gold. Far off, on the other side of the main island, The Bridge of Hope connected the mainland island containing Ma'on, Zebul, Raki'a, and Wilon to a smaller island, Makon. There the angel Etán worked in God's storehouses.

Etán was known for having the strength of many angels. His neck was as large as his thigh, and his arms were the size of his head.

As he shoveled hailstones into an enormous bin below, he couldn't help but wonder why God would want to store hailstones weighing 75–100 pounds each. Since it was not his job to question, he shoveled. However; he concluded there was one good thing about his assignment; the more he shoveled the stronger he became.

Etán stopped shoveling to wipe his brow. As he stretched his back he scanned the rows of bins and watched other angels also shoveling. Each bin held something different: blessings, water, fire, and of course, hailstones. The angel Pyro shoveled fire while Aqua filled a bin with water.

Unlike Etán, Pyro and Aqua were elemental angels. Pyro emitted flames when excited, but Aqua consisted of a watery substance making him appear almost invisible at times.

Etán thought about why he seemed to like working in these Warehouses. He was a loner among angels. He had even thought about enlisting as a warrior angel but disliked companionship, so he shoveled hailstones.

As he returned to his task, he wondered about this new creation. *Evidently,* he surmised, *they must need hailstones.*

their conversations back and forth, scheduling, directing, instructing, and attending. Lucifer understood none of it.

A primary Atik hovered in front of his face looking at him eye to eye. It drifted side to side with fairy-like wings. Lucifer finally understood he was being given instructions to follow the Atik.

As Lucifer walked through the fog, it drifted apart. The Atik led him to a recessed pool where steps led down to a hot tub roiling with steam. Various Atiks took his robe and left him to soak alone. The steam rolled about his head as he relaxed. He allowed his thoughts to rehearse certain scenes and conversations he imagined might arise once he was presented to the Lord. He had time to rehearse his comments over and over until the Atiks returned and helped him out of his bath. In the place of his heavy ornate robe, he was given a light linen robe.

After the Atiks departed, tall and elegant Lucent angels entered. They appeared to communicate among themselves in an unspoken language and carried unusual vials. Lucifer found himself perfumed in a process of *misting*.

"Where do I find the throne room?" He asked the nearest one, hoping the Lucent would be able to understand him.

"You do not go to God," the creature answered in a solemn guttural voice. "God comes to you."

Lucifer chose to ask no further questions. No communication took place until he was informed the time had come. He stretched his neck in uneasiness as the Atiks ushered him toward a circle on the floor. Although the wait was short, Lucifer found it uncomfortable. A cherub appeared and urged him to stand on the circle Lucifer had surmised was for decoration only. The circle was made with inlaid wood of three crosses and, at its center, a large decorative "N" denoted the exact spot of "True North."

Lucifer watched as smoke came from the outside edge of this now cloudy circle.

"Step here, the angel urged, pointing to the inner part of the circle. The smoke began rising at an alarming rate, quicker and quicker, higher and higher, swirling about in the shape of a cylinder. "With haste! With haste!" they pressed, this time with imperative forcefulness.

Lucifer stepped in quickly. He immediately felt the force of vorticular winds gathering in fierce strength, pressing him into a singular dimension. He felt as though he were turning in the swirling winds of a tornado. He lifted his arms to protect his face and head.

Araboth
Chapter Eleven

Turning and churning, curling and twisting, the winds continued their ferocity until he finally felt their strength faltering. As Lucifer relaxed, he drew in an aroma of captivating incense. Chants from afar with canticles of tenor voices in worship caught his ear. The scenery seemed to snap in place, panel by panel, around him.

He found himself standing on a sea of glass. Underneath the glass, fire danced on moving waters.

A creature approached. "The Sea below is the masses of sinless men made pure by the blood of the Lamb and by the fire of the Spirit."

Lucifer understood not a word of the strange statement. The creature led him across the floor where he was met with a Light so intense it blazed across his face, so bright he could not look up. Both he and the creature cast their faces to the floor. Lucifer knew he was in the presence of the Omnipotent God.

Elevated, sitting high upon a throne, His robe of authority filled the room. On His head He wore many crowns on which were written many names: Mighty God, Prince of Peace, Counselor, Everlasting Father.

The image of God was burnt into Lucifer's mind like a laser beam even though Lucifer could not gaze upon His presence. The crystal floor reflected the Light of God's Glory. Acting as a prism, the floor cast a rainbow behind the throne. There were aspects of God Lucifer could see and aspects he could not see. The rainbow seemed to represent the visible form of an invisible God.

Dark clouds displaying a supernatural atomic power filled the room with thunder and lightning.

Above and behind the throne Tinkers hovered, each with six wings, their heads lowered in humility.

Lucifer watched even though he could not look up or speak. Terror had entered his being. His knees and neck were weak and he fell upon his face. He heard a roar, like a waterfall rumbling inside a cavernous enclosure.

Lucifer's Assignment
Chapter Twelve

From within the cavernous enclosure came the voice of the LORD. "Son of the Morning, created in perfection, filled with all beauty and knowledge . . ."

Lucifer remained limp and speechless. He felt as though his being were woven together by nothing more than whispers of air, easily scattered in a puff of wind, his strength nonexistent.

". . . anointed as the protector and guardian of men," the voice of the Lord spoke.

Lucifer felt a touch and was strengthened. Power had been infused into him. As he stood, a rush, like the rush of many winds blowing, blew the scenery away, bringing into view a new landscape – one he did not recognize.

"Lift up your eyes, Lucifer," the voice of the LORD commanded.

Lucifer looked around. Evidently he had been transported to a place he did not recognize. He saw a river rushing before him, separating a left bank from a right bank. Solid rocks jutted above the water, and between the rocks, awash in the vitality of the flowing, living water, two bubbles clung one to the other, dancing in unison upon the waters. They were airy, light and ethereal. Lucifer understood these to be the souls of the one named Adam and the one named Eve.

"This is the River of the Living. These souls are yours to protect and guard." The voice of the LORD rumbled over the roar of the waters. "These are the seeds of the nations that will become the kingdoms of the world, for it will be written that a people yet to be created may praise the LORD."

Lucifer found his feeble voice. "Why do their souls not reside in their bodies?"

"Their souls have no physical dimensions; therefore they have no 'place of position' in their physical world. Rather, they are bubbles that float upon the water in the *River of the Living*. The body knows the soul, and the soul knows the body. If the body hurts, the soul knows its pain. And when the soul hurts, the body is diminished."

"May I ask, O LORD, how long this assignment is to last?" Lucifer asked, stuttering.

"Until the time of the end when those you have protected become joint-heirs and rulers. I leave you this gift: You and you alone as the administrating Archangel of Heaven have access to man's thirteenth dimension of rest. Upon entering, you may offer man a libation of sweet dreams and good rest. Return to your place, Son of the Morning. If you do well, your reward will follow."

The scenery faded away. Lucifer found himself encapsulated in the same swirling cylinder of wind and smoke that originally transported him to the throne room. (*Or had it brought the throne room to him?*) For Lucifer, it was as though the floor had fallen out from under him. In a sudden jerk he collapsed in the circle that had given him entrance to the throne room in the first place; except now, he was disheveled and spent.

His ears burned. *Did what just happen truly happen? Did God indeed say these men would become JOINT-HEIRS and RULERS?* An envious anger welled up in his throat. God had not only promoted man to rule, but demoted him, Lucifer, to being a caretaker for men who were to rule *with* God! His head reeled in confusion and anger. His expectations shattered like exploding glass, shooting shards of pointed pain which shredded his ego and left him wounded with slivers of misery that infected his mind.

As he tried to collect himself, Atiks darted back and forth, offering him a libation to aid in the recovery of his strength. Lucifer refused the drink. In spite of his weakened condition, he snatched up his neatly folded robe and stormed out in a menacing state, wishing to have nothing to do with any creature.

Outside the temple doors, Lucifer noticed Zuben and Menkib were absent, evidently relieved of their duties for the time being. Just as well, for he was in no mood for social dribbling. An angry Lucifer was making plans...BIG PLANS.

Foreboding
Chapter Thirteen

Auroran, just leaving the Honorarium, stared at the heaven's sky, puzzled. The sky, normally filled with orbs and streaks of light, was dark. He had never seen dark clouds, except in rumors describing Araboth, until now.

As he looked, he noticed other angels throughout the heavens had ceased their tasks and were also staring upward. A strange silence filled the heavens.

Auroran remembered a book *A Study on the Eternal Nature of God* describing the creation of the Heavens. He hastily returned to the Honorarium to look for it. Upon finding it, he flipped through the pages until he discovered something he had remembered reading. *Here it is*, he thought as he read:

> "He made darkness canopies around Him, Dark waters and thick clouds of the skies, He made darkness His secret place; His canopy around Him was dark waters and thick clouds of the skies."

Auroran remembered temple angels describing the power of the Almighty. Auroran picked his way through his thoughts. *Perhaps,* he reasoned, *God's creation could not comprehend such power, and such darkness expressed the creation's fear of the Lord.*

This must be an omen of something amiss. Auroran shuddered.

Big Plans
Chapter Fourteen

Lucifer was oblivious to time as he withdrew, doing only those duties which were absolutely required. He spent most of his days sulking after yet another humiliating defeat. He had a plan, but he needed Zuben's assistance.

"What do you mean you got lost and fell through the universe?" Zuben asked, rather shocked.

"Shhh!!!" Lucifer sternly warned his friend. "It's demoralizing!"

"How did it feel?" Zuben prodded, in a lower voice, now in profound curiosity.

"I felt utter terror, abandoned to the deepest of emptiness, swallowed whole by imploding darkness. A force grabbed me without warning. It stretched me out as it pulled me through a worm hole. I was strung into a long beam of light not knowing up from down." Lucifer knitted his brow. "The stress created a forced rest that melted me into liquid light. My being became an abandoned, floating dollop of light. It was *not* a pleasant experience."

Zuben saw the terror in Lucifer's pale face. "Give yourself credit," Zuben encouraged him. "You forged ahead where no other angel would dare to go. Look what you've achieved!" Zuben was astonished at Lucifer's boldness in his attempt to reach man's earth. Although Zuben was known for his courage, still he would never have taken such a maiden voyage.

"I may need your help," Lucifer confessed, mentally gauging Zuben's reactions.

Zuben sat back, stupefied; *never in his angelic life had Lucifer come to him for help.*

"I *must* get there," Lucifer insisted. "I will *find* a way or *make* a way." he paused. "Is your answer 'yes' or 'no?'"

"What is it you want from me, my friend?" Zuben replied. "You know whatever you ask it is my duty to help, and to help fearlessly."

Lucifer dismissed his attendants and before sharing his plans with Zuben in privacy. "From the arena in the mount," Lucifer instructed, "direct me as I go. You know here, in the heavens, I have the capacity to see all that is around me, but once I enter this aberrant universe, I no longer have oversight. All I can see is that which is in front of me. Will you help?"

"Of course, my friend," Zuben answered. "You know I will. But one question: Has the Almighty agreed to this?"

"He has not said 'No,'" Lucifer replied. He grabbed both of Zuben's hands and shook them to secure his pledge.

As they walked together to the arena, Lucifer described even more of his plummeting, erratic ride through the universe as Zuben listened in awe.

When they reached the arena, at Lucifer's urging, Zuben stood by Corona ready to serve.

"Once I reach earth," Lucifer instructed, "you may leave the arena. There will be no further need to keep you from your other duties."

"Now, how do we communicate?" Zuben asked once again, to make sure he understood perfectly.

"Broadband ... focus on the beam of light," Lucifer scowled.

"OK." Zuben was ready.

Take Off
Chapter Fifteen

Lucifer stepped up and on the ring of fire to slip through the bubble one leg at a time, just as he had done before. This time, however, he was ready to stabilize himself. He knew how to expand and soar. After a last-minute preflight check, he was ready to receive Zuben's directions.

The instant his legs were inside Corona, he fired off like a rocket, traveling many times faster than the speed of light. As he rocketed through the universe he could not help but wonder: *What would these men think if they could see their own universe?*

As Lucifer traveled from galaxy to galaxy, Zuben navigated for him. Sometimes the communication failed, but when Lucifer was within light, they were able to communicate clearly once again.

The trip was exhausting, but finally Lucifer saw the earth come into view. He landed gently in the Garden of Eden, just as he had planned. "I have arrived," he announced to Zuben.

"My congratulations," Zuben offered. "You did it." He then signed off.

Yes, I did it! Lucifer congratulated himself. Hardly able to contain his excitement, he walked upon the grasses in the cool of the evening, basking in the remaining rays of golden sunlight. A soft breeze cooled his face. He enjoyed the earth's temperature, light, and beauty. The canopy of ice around the orb of the earth shielded all life from the damaging rays of the sun and served as a hyperbaric chamber feeding oxygen to proliferating plants. Cells self-generated endlessly. A tropical mist rose from the chambers beneath the crust of the earth watering this abundant garden. Lucifer breathed deeply. He leaned against a tree and relaxed. His only companions were his thoughts. *This creation is as perfect as "shevah," the root of the number seven.* Lucifer thought about how seven represented the perfection of God. *Just like the number seven, His creation was full and complete, good, and full of perfection. Nothing could be added to it or taken from it without marring it.* Try as he might, Lucifer could find no fault in it.

Remembering his mission, his pleasant thoughts quickly turned bitter. *God had set eternity in the heart of man, and man would live into eternity. Unfortunately,* Lucifer grumbled, *they are here to stay.*

As he grumbled, Lucifer turned and saw something unexpected. Beyond a stand of trees, God, in the form of a man, walked with Adam and

Eve. They strolled together beneath a bough-covered pathway in the cool of the evening, all of one mind. The angels had never been this close to God. God's friendship with man was an intimacy Lucifer could not tolerate.

After all his years of serving God faithfully, after working diligently for God's approval, God had now replaced him with a new, favorite son. Lucifer had always tried to win God's favor by his work. Now he felt unappreciated, shaken, undone, rattled. *Nothing like this had been witnessed before. Who is man that God should esteem him so? What is it about this creature that captivates the heart of God?* At once, a consuming rage ignited causing a billowing and churning within. Like papers in a fire, his hands curled into fists.

A gust of wind came up as though to scatter his rage around him. It lifted his hair over his head causing it to dance in the wind, capturing the reflecting red rays of the setting sun.

Lucifer raised his fist from earth to Heaven: "I will ascend above the heights of the clouds of angels; I will ascend into the seventh Heaven in *Araboth*. I will exalt *my* throne above the stars of God, I will sit upon the mount of the congregation in *Ma'on*, and in the side of the north, in God's temple in *Zebul* – *I* will be like the most High."

A plan materialized: *If he could convince Eve to disobey Adam, and Adam to disobey God, then with one act, he could take mankind out of the presence of the most holy God forever.*

The Fall of Man
Chapter Sixteen

Lucifer waited patiently in the Garden of Eden for Eve to stray from Adam. Fearing she might drop everything and run if he suddenly approached the woman, who was not aware of his existence, he looked for an animal he could indwell.

By his good fortune Eve walked next to the tree of good and evil in the middle of the Garden. He spied the resourceful serpent basking in the sun on one of its tree limbs. *I will indwell the serpent and deceive the woman! Now,* he decided, *is the time to strike.*

Through the serpent, his voice called out to Eve, "Did God *really* say, 'You must not eat from *any* tree in the garden?'"

Eve was perfectly comfortable responding to the serpent. "We may indeed eat fruit from the trees in the Garden, but God did warn Adam saying,

'You must not eat fruit from the tree in the middle of the Garden,' the tree you are now basking in," Eve continued, "and He warned us not to even touch the tree, or we would die.'"

The serpent scoffed at Eve's stern warning. "You will *not* surely die!" He coiled himself around the branch of the tree to illustrate he was not *just* touching the tree, but *hugging* it! "God knows when you eat this delicious fruit your eyes will be opened, and you will be like God, knowing both good *and evil*." He hit one of the ripe fruits knocking it off the tree. It bounced off Eve's shoulder before landing on the ground.

"The fruit touched me and I did not die!" Eve exclaimed.

"Of course not," the serpent replied. "It is as I said."

"It looks pleasant enough." She picked it up and examined it, turning it over and over in her hand.

Seth, the lamb, butted her to warn her, but the sticky nectar of the luscious fruit was already dripping between her fingers. She touched her tongue to it and found it quite delectable. When Eve found the fruit of the tree tasted good, that it was pleasing to look at, and also desirable for gaining wisdom, she took a bite. When she bit down, into the core, she discovered that the fruit caused her to realize things she had never seen before.

The lamb's antics caught Adam's eye and he came to see what was happening. He was carrying beautiful flowers because he had learned how flowers pleased Eve. When he saw Eve eating the fruit he was alarmed. The flowers fell to the earth. Although he ran, crushing the flowers, it was too late to stop her.

"Here, Adam, I ate and I did not die. See?"

It was true. Eve had not died. Adam hesitated.

"Wow!" Eve exclaimed. "Can you see what I see?"

Adam took the fruit Eve handed him and, very slowly, he took a bite.

She and Adam both stared at their changed world.

"You are naked." Eve had never realized this and felt shame.

"You are, too," Adam said, pointed out her shame as well as his.

Their eyes were opened, and they realized they were naked. So they sewed fig leaves together and made coverings for themselves.

"If God was not truthful when He told us we would die," Eve asked, "I wonder what else He is hiding from us?"

"Why should God have to tell us His secrets?" Adam scowled.

A Quake
Chapter Seventeen

In heaven a quake hit!

The winds of heaven blew like a storm. The weather vane at the top of the Honorarium spun out of control. The foundations of the heavens shook sideways as bewildered angels stared at each other, unaware of what had just transpired on earth. The Stones of Fire, the very foundations of Heaven, rumbled from their place.

Auroran knew the earthquake must have something to do with the dark clouds. Now he was truly alarmed. The clouds were a harbinger of the earthquake. He winced as he looked around wondering whether there was more to come.

Angels rushed to the arena in search of the cause of the quake, but Corona revealed nothing on earth. Everything was just as it had been. Not a leaf was out of place (except for a few fig leaves Adam and Eve had donned). They could see nothing that would cause concern.

The angels did not perceive the real damage on earth, which happened where the River of the Living ran through the bowels of the earth, the place God had shown Lucifer. Two iridescent souls now floated in darkness upon a compromised river. The quake had shaken the entire eleventh dimension of the Spirit World, from the top of the heavens down to the bowels of the earth. Two souls, once immersed in light, now saw only the dark nakedness of the other. This nakedness gave each one ample reason to criticize the other. They were no longer oblivious to evil.

The quake split the River of the Living wide open. In the channel where Living Water once flowed, a flood of foul fluid now filled a newly formed chasm. As the fluid spilled in, it thoroughly tainted the souls of men, polluting their opaline purity with a virus of sin. Soft, round bubbles became hardened and skewed, creating a distortion of life and truth. This "virus" permanently altered the spiritual DNA within their souls. Normally the size of a fist; pride, like yeast, caused their souls to swell and double in size. Puffed up and turgid, the swelling of the soul cut off man's source of power to God.

The spirit within the soul withered and died. Irreparable damage was done to the soul, but with the spirit now dead, man was indeed doomed. His body would eventually die as it used up its source of power, but since his soul was created to live eternally, man became the walking dead - having an eternal soul and a dead spirit.

No Other Rock
Chapter Eighteen

God had warned Adam and Eve, but they did not understand the depth of the consequences of their disobedience. Without Him as their source of power, the cells in their bodies no longer self-generated endlessly. Their bodies would eventually die, even though their eternal souls lived forever – hopelessly, in darkness.

At the onslaught of the quake, the River of the Living had been rerouted through Sheol.

God, in Araboth, knew all that would happen before He created men. Nothing that occurred caught God by surprise. The Ancient of Days already knew the end from the beginning. After all, He had a plan.

One side of the river God called *Hades*, the other side, *Paradise*. In Paradise He set up an outpost of Heaven called *Shehaqim*. Paradise, like Heaven, was a place of rest. Together, Hades and Paradise were known as *Sheol*, the place of the dead.

Upon the river, souls once bobbing up and down in living water now rode a slick of sludge in a sin-filled slough. Both the body and the soul, separated from God, had but one destiny, the grave.

God knew from then forward, when man's body died it would decompose in a physical grave returning to the dirt from which it was made. Man's soul, however, would detach and separate from other souls in the River of the Living. Depending on the remaining light in the soul, it would float either to the Paradise or to the Hades side of the river.

God grieved from above. Mourning for Lucifer, God cried out, "You were the seal of perfection, full of wisdom and perfect in beauty. You were in Eden, the garden of God; like a rare and valuable necklace, every precious stone adorned you. Your settings and mountings were made of gold; on the day you were created they were prepared. You were anointed as a guardian cherub, for so I ordained you...."

God saw Lucifer's heart. A prickly vine of envy had taken hold in a rich, well-fertilized soil of pride, growing and twisting, choking out his wisdom and beauty.

The heart of the Lord God folded in grief as He concluded of Lucifer: "You were blameless in your ways from the day you were created ... until iniquity was found in you."

God knew his walks in the Garden with His creation had come to an end. A connective cohesion no longer existed between God and man. Man's spirit was dead. Man was now alone and lost in his mental solitary confinement. In spite of all that had happened, God did not forget His Pact: All that had been decided would be done, and all that He foreknew would certainly come to pass.

God even knew Lucifer was now in Heaven creating an uproar among the angels with deceptive rumors.

If God were man, he might have wondered if *any* of His creatures, angels *or* men, would choose to trust Him. But being God, the Alpha and Omega, the beginning and the end, the First and the Last, He knew from before the foundation of the worlds all that would take place –from the majestic to the minutia; from the mysteries in the Days of Old to the mysteries in the Ages to Come. For God declared of Himself: "I am God – I only – and there is no other like me who can tell you all that is going to happen. All I say will come to pass, for I do whatever I wish. Is there a God besides Me? Indeed *there is* no other Rock; I know not one.'"

Consequences
Chapter Nineteen

Auroran went to the arena for more information on the quake and the upheaval. He was not surprised to find a bustling bevy of angels peering into Corona as it floated upon its ring of fire. "What is it? What's happening?"

"Shh!" an angel whispered. "The Lord God is cursing the serpent of the earth."

"Cursing the serpent? Why?" Auroran tried to see over the heads of the others.

"Shh! Listen. Something called *Sin*."

He leaned into the crowd in order to hear. God was indeed speaking to the serpent:

"I will put war between you and the woman, and between your seed and her seed; her seed shall bruise you on the head, and you shall bruise her seed on the heel."

Auroran watched and listened as God turned to Eve. "I will make your pains in childbearing severe. Furthermore, your desire will be for your husband, and he will rule over you."

"What does that mean?" Auroran asked.

"Shh! Listen ... please!" Many angels were straining to hear. "God is now speaking to Adam!"

"In the sweat of your face you shall eat bread until you return to the ground, for out of it you were taken. Dust you *are,* and to dust you shall return."

Auroran quibbled. "I thought God had set eternity in the heart of man. How, then, can man return to the ground?"

"I see you are as confused as I," an angel whispered. "What is your name?"

"Auroran," he replied. "And you?"

"Kasdaye," his counterpart answered. "These men are strange creatures, are they not? I cannot fathom their value."

Kasdaye and Marcus
Chapter Twenty

Kasdaye pondered this mankind to see what role men might play in his own future. He revisited the Honorarium to see if there was something about them worth his study. He picked up a scroll aimlessly.

As the angel of signs and wonders he held a prestigious position in the Heavens. Lucifer often called upon him to perform the impossible. At creation he assisted with placing stars in man's heavens for seasons, signs, and wonders.

Kasdaye knew who he was, for God had made him with the ability to create atmospheres and impressions with a wave of his hands. Whenever he used his hands they would leave a trail of sparkles. He stood out among the angels not only in his mannerisms but in his dress, sporting a hat and a goatee.

He enjoyed using his talent to motivate large hosts of angels at assemblies, moving them toward positive outcomes.

He spied Borealis in the Honorarium. "Ho! Borealis."

"Kasdaye." Borealis turned and greeted him.

The two angels touched arms.

"I see you are studying," Borealis commented nonchalantly.

"I am," Kasdaye replied. He was just about to share his thoughts on mankind when he noticed something unusual in Borealis. "How are you my friend? Is something amiss?"

Borealis was unusually antsy. "I guess I'm seeking something," Borealis replied, "but I don't know what."

The double doors of the Honorarium opened and Marcus entered. "Kasdaye!" he exclaimed. "I was looking for you."

Kasdaye and Marcus often worked together since Marcus was the angel of pleasures.

Kasdaye introduced Marcus to Borealis.

Borealis thought both angels exuded great charm. They were handsome, each in his own way, while Kasdaye was outgoing, Marcus was reserved.

The two angels chatted while Borealis sighed.

Kasdaye turned his attention to Borealis. "What's is it?"

"I need an assignment, something that would require my passion," Borealis murmured.

"You will find it or it will find you," Kasdaye laughed.

Marcus likewise encouraged Borealis with intriguing thoughts of possible adventures.

Borealis felt encouraged as he left the two angels, who were now engrossed in conversation about God's new creation.

The Cavern of Hades
Chapter Twenty-One

Lucifer, wrapped in his cape, swirled about in the darkness of his newfound cavern. *How does God like His mankind, His prodigal son NOW?!* He laughed and felt a surge of satisfaction from getting his revenge. As he reveled in his demented glee, he wandered through various openings of the cavern until he stumbled upon a cathedral filled with fingerlike pillars. Lofty and menacing, they pointed 700 feet upwards, piercing the hollowness of the cavern. An eerie incandescent glow cast irreligious shadows across the floors and walls.

Lucifer reasoned that since God is light, in this place of utter, abysmal darkness, he would be invisible to God's oversight. Furthermore, the fact that God had taken no action against him further confirmed he was correct.

Filled with exuberance, Lucifer shouted, "I am the god of this world!" His voice resonated within the cavern.

Long yellow stalagmites, fangs in the rotting mouth of mother earth, hung from the lofty ceiling along the walls. They echoed back to him in strange vibrating tones. "I AM the god of this world... I Am the god... I am... I am... i am...."

Unbeknownst to Lucifer, his cavern was located on the Hades side of Sheol. Far back a maze-like tunnel opened onto a dark beachhead where a path led to the River of the Living, the same River of the Living God had revealed to Lucifer in Heaven. Across the river was Paradise. On the far side of Paradise was Shehaqim, an outpost of heaven.

The compromised River of the Living threaded its way through the bottom of a chasm separating Hades from Paradise.

Lucifer had been so preoccupied with his vision for his future he didn't notice the sounds of the river. Continuing his exploration of the cathedral, he found a smaller cavern, well-suited for setting up his war room. He walked around the envisioned war room, measuring it with his steps.

Here, in the bowels of the earth, Lucifer thought smugly, *I am free to carry out my objectives, unknown and unseen in Heaven.*

Lucifer sized up God's position: God **must** destroy mankind because of man's disobedience.

If He doesn't, He has compromised His own righteousness within the Laws of Heaven and would be forced to step down from His throne.

On the other hand, God **cannot** destroy man since He promised him a redeemer, one who would bruise his, Lucifer's, head. Destroying man would make God a liar. Being a liar was also contrary to God's character written within the laws and ordinances of Heaven. If God were found to lie, that would also force Him to step down from His throne.

Either way, Lucifer concluded, *God could no longer be a holy, righteous, and hallowed God.*

Now, he thought, *anything* God does or does not do will compromise the Laws and Ordinances of Heaven causing the foundations of Heaven to crack and crumble. Lucifer reasoned that God's only choice was to defect from His throne. All Lucifer had to do was force God's hand.

He smiled. Throughout his career as an administrator, he had spent his time studying the Laws of Heaven; he was the only angel who realized *God could be trapped by His own self-made Laws.* After all, God was in subjugation to His own character. He could not be untrue to Himself.

Lucifer chuckled. The conflict in God between His love for His creation and His holy righteousness would be His undoing.

Lucifer was smug. He had outsmarted God and therefore, he was wiser than God.

Lucifer pulled a prized possession from his pocket – an illegally obtained copy of Auroran's key to the future. As the administrator of Heaven, Lucifer had instructed Acamar to get him a copy of this key with orders to keep it a secret. After the three angels left the vault, he snuck in behind them and used the key to watch the future open before his eyes where he saw himself ruling over the heavens!

I've already won! Lucifer gloried.

God's Perspective
Chapter Twenty-Two

From the Temple on the Mount, God not only saw Lucifer in his cavern but read every diabolical intention of his heart.

His archangel had underestimated Him. Even before He created angels or men, everything had been determined.

Only One such as *HE* was able to look down the hallway of time to see ALL possible futures. As God, He alone saw all possible choices made by all possible beings. And was it not He alone who chose the outcome He desired – the one and only pathway that would give men and angels complete free will but with the outcome He chose?

Being God, He and He alone secured one future against all others.

If only Lucifer had understood that if he had only accepted God's appointment to be the guardian of men, if he had done right by man, God would have promoted Lucifer to rule over the Heavens. But neither angel nor man understood His plans. As God, He did not explain Himself or defend His actions to men, to angels, or to any creature in Heaven or on earth below.

Of Himself, He declared, "I am God – I only – and there is no other like me who can tell you what is going to happen. The past, the present, and the future are all mine, one and the same. That which has been decided will come to be." *No, Son of the Morning, I will not destroy my creation because you corrupted them with your weeds of rebellion. No, I will wait until the harvest. Then all men will be gathered together to the Great White Throne Judgment. This gathering is my crop. There, the weeds of rebellion will be separated from the wheat of faithfulness. I will gather my faithful, like wheat, into my barn. But the unfaithful, those weeds of rebellion, will be gathered and burnt in the furnace.*

Therefore, know this day, and consider it in your heart, there is no other God besides Me. I am the First and I am the Last; besides Me there is no God. Have I not declared it? Indeed there is no other Rock of Truth; I know not one.

Rumors
Chapter Twenty-Three

"Zuben and Menkib!" Borealis gleefully called out as his foot touched the earth. "You two are here? Is this an assignment?"

The two muscular angels, facing each other at the entrance to the Garden of Eden, held their flaming swords firmly in their hands, each muscle contracting and expanding as the swords flashed and turned. They were surprised to see another angel and delighted it was Borealis.

"We are commanded to keep Adam and Eve from returning to the Garden of Eden, to keep them from eating from the Tree of Life. I volunteered you," Zuben laughed. "But you were nowhere to be found."

Borealis joined their laughter. "I was eager to explore this dynamic universe! Did you know there are over 100 billion galaxies, that the earth spins 1,000 miles per hour, and that the earth travels through space at 67,000 miles per hour?" Borealis paused, cocked his head. "But wait, what do you mean 'Adam and Eve cannot return to the Garden.' I'm confused." Borealis frowned. "First, God creates man and puts him in the Garden – then, Adam and Eve are evicted?"

"To be honest," Zuben answered, "I'm a little confused myself. Man lost his dominion over the earth and Lucifer laid a quitclaim deed to it. Yes, it's very confusing. I want to complete this assignment and return to Ma'on as soon as possible. But, we have no idea how long this assignment will last."

Borealis nodded in agreement that he too was eager to return to the city of God. "Have you seen Lucifer?"

"Only rumors," Zuben answered, "and only more things I do not understand."

"I've also heard many things," Menkib interjected. "Mostly that Lucifer has rebelled."

"Rebelled?!" Borealis exclaimed. "How do you rebel against the Almighty?" Borealis was in shock. He knew he must return to the Mount immediately. *Rebellion? Can such a thing be done?* He knew he must see his brother. Surely Auroran would dispel these unbelievable rumors. He turned and spoke to his friends: "I am returning to Ma'on." He paused before saying, "I know the two of you can't leave, but at least I can come back with facts, not rumors."

"Please ask if Lucifer has indeed rebelled," Zuben implored. "I *am* his closest associate."

"I'm eager for *any* news!" Menkib interjected.

As Borealis prepared to leave, a rustling in the bushes distracted him. He stopped and stared. There was the man Adam reaching across a patch of thorns for berries. The man was smaller than he had envisioned. His hair was dirty and unkempt and his arms red with scratches from the thorns. Borealis stared at him. "I have not seen man in the flesh before."

"He and Eve do not look well," Zuben added.

"Can he see us?" Borealis asked.

"He could if we folded into his dimension," Menkib explained, "and if we did, we would appear to him as other men, but that is not allowed, not without the express consent of God."

"He can't see us," Zuben continued. "But we can see him. To men we are nothing more than a streak of light here or a beam of light there. We move far too fast for them to see us. Man can only perceive four of his 13 dimensions. He is utterly blind to our eleventh dimension and his spirit world."

Borealis sniffed the air. "What is that foul odor that surrounds us?"

"That, my friend, is the stench of *Sin*!" Menkib chimed in. "It's the spray of rebellion. I find traces of it throughout the Garden. I can hardly bear it myself."

Borealis' nose wrinkled in objection to the odor. "...Well, I will return as soon as possible with whatever news I can gather." Borealis gave each angel his forearm.

"Surely!" Zuben and Menkib replied simultaneously. "Godspeed!"

Borealis ascended. He watched Zuben and Menkib fade from view below. The enjoyment of his adventures had ceased. *Surely, these rumors cannot be true.*

Civil War!
Chapter Twenty-Four

Auroran felt the weight of keys jangling on his waistband as he hustled to the Honorarium. "Breeze ... come." A small breeze appeared to cool his flushed face.

Lucifer had rebelled! Who would have believed such a thing? Far back, before creation, when Auroran had been given a key to a bottomless pit, he inquired of God about its meaning. The answer God gave was: "If the LORD creates a new thing, and the earth opens its mouth and swallows them up with all that belong to them, and they go down alive into the pit, then you will understand that these have rejected the LORD." At the time, he had not understood. But now, with these current events, he began to see an unnerving picture of an ominous future.

Auroran composed himself upon entering the rotunda of the Honorarium and quietly took a seat. Here he could concentrate on writing his assignment, a report on the recent events concerning men and angels. He had to record it, record it all.

Each word must measure the exact weight of its significance, create an understanding of pure truth to explain the unfathomable value of God's essence. Mixed together, this was the inkwell of God's golden glory. Into this inkwell Auroran dipped his quill.

Under normal circumstances, Auroran would have guided it across the pages of the scroll, directing it with the soft touches of a master, letting it dance upon the paper. Instead, the quill trembled in his hand. He understood the implications of his report:

> "By the will of God and in His Service, I, Auroran, the angel in whom God has entrusted the keys of heaven and hell, the bottomless pit, the past and the future, do heretofore set my hand to journal the following accounts concerning these present events of men and angels:
>
> Lucifer is in rebellion, declaring an unholy war against the Almighty. Even now, on the far shores of the heavenly realm, beyond the mountain of God, dark clouds gather. In such I see an ominous foreboding of that which is to come. Lucifer pontificates an inglorious message in an attempt to recruit all who might believe his delirious accusations.
>
> It has been reported that his countenance no longer reflects the glory of God but, rather, magnifies its own darkness.
>
> Likewise; mankind has fallen. Being taken captive, they have become the walking dead – indestructible souls destined for an everlasting life of death. Their one decision led them through a gate of consequences from which there is no return.
>
> Man's disobedience has created an earthquake in the landscape of the irredeemable future. The days of man's physical life are now enclosed between the two eternities. Yet, even so, eternity has been set in the heart of man such that man's heart beats with an everlasting hope – against all hope.
>
> Angels who once eagerly gazed upon the universe, full of newness, excitement, intrigue, and the mystique of mankind now avoid the arena. They have no understanding concerning

man's eviction from the Garden or this concept called 'sin.' They wonder if they will be affected personally. A curse covers the earth. It is difficult to watch the hopelessness and suffering that now pervade mankind and everything in his environment.

Angels are questioning God's wisdom in creating this mankind. 'Why,' they ask, 'would God choose to make man when, in His eternal knowledge, He knew that man would be hopelessly damned?'"

Auroran stopped and sighed. Heaviness overtook him. He forced himself to see the possible unsavory conclusions of his report. He dipped his quill in his inkwell and continued:

"Civil war in heaven is imminent.

Since Lucifer has blinded man to true values, the angels Wisdom and Choices are assigned to earth to aid mankind. Wisdom assigns each item, relationship, and event a spiritual value so that a man is able to weigh his options while Choices carries the scale upon which those choices can be weighed.

God has built a hedge of protection around the two angels such that they may roam the earth without being accosted by Lucifer.

Alas, this day will be remembered throughout the eternities as a day of grief and a day of sorrow.

While all things are uncertain, I, Auroran, have been instructed to lock away the keys to the future. In this I dutifully oblige.

I swear by Him who lives forever and forever that this report is just and true. Power and Glory and Honor to Him who was, and is, and is to come, the Almighty.

His Dutiful Servant, Auroran"

The Secret Things
Chapter Twenty-Five

Auroran titled and sealed his report, the first of many to come. As his seal hardened he noticed a new plaque on the wall above the arched entrance of the Honorarium: *"The Secret Things belong to the LORD our God."* Auroran puzzled over its meaning, but was quickly diverted by various Books of Antiquity on the shelf catching his eye: *The Physics and Laws of the Heavenly Realm, The Songs of the Angels, The Secrets of the Ages Past,* among others.

He had to remind himself he was in the Honorarium for reasons other than writing his report. First, he had earned one session with the Tinker, OKUL. He could ask OKUL any question and OKUL would answer with God-given insight. Second, God had given Auroran the task of choosing a float of angels to act as scribes for two new books – the *Book of Life* and the *Chronicles of Men*. Auroran wanted to give this assignment to his brother. *Too bad this task would be nothing his impetuous brother might be interested in.* He longed to see his twin, but Borealis had not been seen in an inordinate amount of time. The fact that Borealis' absence coincided with Lucifer's rebellion created concern in Auroran that Borealis might be either intrigued by this rebellion or even involved. Such a concern lay heavy at the bottom of his heart.

Deep in thought, Auroran startled when he heard the angel D'shubba's voice behind him.

"Greetings, Auroran."

As the Overseer of the Honorarium, D'shubba's square cap covered his bald head and trailed down his back. It was adorned with names, badges, and medallions earned for his outstanding service to the Lord. Other angels wore their service medallions on their armbands in tiny chains of jewelry, but none had quite as many as D'shubba. Such identifications of honor were highly prized and not earned easily. D'shubba, as was his custom, walked with his hands tucked inside the opposite sleeves of his robe.

"What news this day?" D'shubba inquired. "There are many rumors as you well know."

"Some are not rumors," Auroran replied, shaking his head solemnly.

"So it is true." D'shubba paused. "Lucifer has rebelled?"

"Yes, my friend. It is as you say. On the far shores of the Heavens he tries to recruit angels, only to retreat when he is discovered. He then escapes to hide inside the universe of man."

D'shubba's eyebrows arched in surprise. "Have other angels followed him?"

"None of whom I am aware." Auroran paused before adding: "But man has fallen." What more could Auroran say? The temporary silence between them created a path of grief that seemed to say it all.

D'shubba led Auroran to a place where they could talk in private. "Can you explain this bottomless pit in which the Lord God has given you the keys? I don't fully understand it."

"I can only share what I understand. It is a place of emptiness where enough is never enough. A worm of neediness gnaws in eternal circles." Auroran struggled to explain it. "It is incompleteness. It cries out: 'More, more, more....'" Auroran paused. "It is like being hungry for something you cannot have." The thought of such a place made him quiver.

"I cannot fathom this Auroran. I do not understand hunger." D'shubba brows crossed in perplexity.

Auroran tried to approach his explanation differently. "The number seven represents God; it is perfect, full, complete, and satisfied. The number six, however, is incompleteness. It comes short of satisfaction and represents neediness. The faces of the needy cry out for more, but more is never enough. Since only God can satisfy the needs of man, then man, without God, remains forever needy."

"Then it is a mathematical equation without a solution?" D'shubba frowned. "This leaves me very troubled."

"Yes," Auroran sighed. "Without the One True God, man is incomplete, unsatisfied, and hurting. He tries to fill his own needs but his eyes are not satisfied with seeing and his ears are not filled with hearing. He fights for things that have no value for reasons that have no meaning. These do not satisfy and leave even more emptiness. There seems to be no solution."

"Is it connected in any way with Lucifer's rebellion?" D'shubba asked.

"Yes. Lucifer caused man to disobey God. Disobedience separated man from God. This leaves man as empty as the bottomless pit. I am confident, however, that the Almighty has a solution, although it is a mystery. We must be patient, for He will reveal it in time."

"I agree," D'shubba said, smiling. They walked back into the rotunda to discuss the float of angels that Auroran must choose. "Have you made a decision as to the scribes to include for the project of recording Man's Chronicles?"

"I am seeking your opinion D'shubba. What do you think about the angel Chronos for his understanding of chronological time, and Kairos for his gift of divine moments?"

"Excellent choices, both of them, but...." D'shubba's voice trailed off.

"But?" Auroran waited.

"Can they be trusted?" A hushed silence punctuated D'shubba's question. He had made his point.

"We shall see.... We shall see." Auroran's voice trailed off. That was all the encouragement he could muster. It was clear that, from here on out, all angels would be under a cloud of suspicion.

"A pending angelic war...," D'shubba murmured as he turned to leave. Their meeting had come to an end.

"Who could have foreseen such a turn of events? From the joy of the creation to ... *this*," Auroran added sadly.

D'shubba paused at the entrance and looked back. "Blessings and Honor, Auroran." Both angels caught the seriousness in the eye of the other. D'shubba put his finger on his forehead then turned it outwards, toward Auroran as a sign of trust.

"Blessings and Honor to you, D'shubba," Auroran said quietly, nodding, but D'shubba was already gone. Auroran's thoughts returned to his brother, wondering, *Where might he be?*

Opius Kele Ursala Lynx
Chapter Twenty-Six

After D'shubba's exit, Auroran sought out OKUL in the *Pane Room*. As a tinker, OKUL, short for Opius Kele Ursala Lynx, was a special angel. He not only shared the eleventh dimension with the spirit world of the angels, he existed in even more dimensions than men or angels. He was full of understanding, although he, like all other angels, did not have access to the strange and volatile thirteenth dimension of men's rest.

"Greetings, Seeker," OKUL said as he appeared in the pane. "What is your question?"

"I desire to know the timing of mankind on earth," Auroran queried.

OKUL nodded. "With the Lord, a thousand years is as one day. The universe began with 'A New Heaven and A New Earth' and it will end with 'A New Heaven and A New Earth.' The end meets the beginning. Man has one thousand man-years for each day of creation and one thousand man-years for the seventh day of rest. Man's last thousand years will be a time of rest, a Sabbath, the Millennium. Man's universe is God's wedding ring, a perfect size seven." OKUL finished. He faded as Auroran contemplated his sayings. They were difficult to understand, but it seemed everything was difficult to understand these days.

Auroran tried again. "How long will mankind last?"

OKUL reappeared. "Forever."

Auroran still understood very little. How could they last forever when their destiny was to be destroyed for disobedience as prescribed by the Laws of Heaven?

His fingertips seem to tickle around the Key to the Future – a key he was forbidden to use. He had not yet locked the two keys away. There was nothing to do but wait and see how all things would play out.

Back in the Honorarium he noticed something awry. *The Pact of the Triune God* was gone. Auroran reasoned that D'shubba must have moved it. He dismissed the anomaly.

Auroran felt weary. He needed to enter into his rest. He left the Honorarium to find a place where he could melt into a pool of liquid light. He followed the layered brick "Path of Life" to an outdoor patio called *Sabaot*, the sleeping ground for angels. It was a place of beauty, a patio of bricks surrounded by greenery –trees, bushes of various colors, and vibrant flowers. Overhead, miniature stars, strung together by cords, twinkled creating an atmosphere of the supernatural. Several tall cylindrical boulders surrounded the patio, each with a deep depression in its top and engraved on the front with the number "8." Some were sparkling, filled with sleeping angels. *When there is rest,* Auroran mused, *there is fulfillment and satisfaction.* He sat on the top of one of the empty boulders and reached upwards for a soothing release. He lifted his arms into the air, stretching, before giving way, melting into liquid light. The boulder encapsulated him in its comforting, strong arms as he slept for an indeterminate length of time. He was awash in ecstasy.

When he returned to his form, he found himself thoroughly refreshed and ready to return to his duties.

Recruiting
Chapter Twenty-Seven

In the cavern, Lucifer realized his plans were proceeding better and faster than he could have possibly anticipated. Adam and Eve's heart, now infected with sin, grew wild with an unnatural bent toward darkness, away from the light. He had succeeded in breaking the bands between God and man.

Now he had to focus on recruiting at least a handful of angels.

He thought back to his recruitment speeches in Heaven: *"What are God's plans for you? Since He intended to make me a servant of man, what intentions does He have for you? What is your future? Do you know? Has He revealed any plans for you or made you promises? Let me ask you this: Have you been His servants ... or His slaves! Am I not right? Show me I am wrong!"*

Lucifer savored the memory of how he had created confusion. His rhetoric gathered like a storm, pulling everything unstable into its path, leaving angels in turmoil.

Imagine God wanting him to be a servant to man! Ha! His indignation rose from his belly into his face. It was assuaged only when he could revel in man's position *now*. Not only had he taken man captive, but he had also stirred the winds of Heaven.

He knew it was critical to acquire a following of angels quickly lest he lose his credibility. He must have something to offer. He sketched out a map of the earth. Mentally, he divided it into segments. He could offer angels control of those segments. *Yes! That was the answer: If he offered choice positions to certain angels, then they could recruit angels under them, then those angels could also recruit – each layer offering something to the angels under them.* He could market and trade on the control of the souls of men! He knew this would work because He remembered how God had told man to multiply and cover the earth. With this information, he could offer the kingdoms of the world to a hierarchy of angels who would report directly to him. These top angels would then divvy up their portions to angels under them in a down line.

He was now prepared to set up the war room to support his vision of his kingdom. He needed a list of angelic hopefuls and, happily, several came to mind.

Leaning back against a porous rock, he relaxed completely until it crumbled and gave way. Lucifer scrambled to sit upright, brushing off various bits of debris and ignoring the omen. He delightfully proclaimed: "In this cavern I will build my House of Royalty!"

He scribbled out his plans. *I will be the god of the earth. The strongest will rule over the weakest; predator and prey will compete in a survival of the fittest. After all, I am the strongest among men and angels. The rulers of the earth will do my good pleasure in exchange for power, greed, and fame.*

Lucifer scribbled his thoughts faster and faster. *Using fear and greed, I have the power to manipulate mankind into doing anything I wish.*

Lucifer knew men would now make decisions based on their own interests – not on the interests of others or the interests of God.

This *is the kingdom that will make me greater than God! Since man is infected with a sin nature, he will do anything to save himself!*

Lucifer looked around, spied a dripping stalactite beneath which a pool had gathered on the ground. He walked over to admire his reflection but his pleasure turned to horror when he saw his reflection. He had withered into something dark and unrecognizable! *"What happened? What happened to my beautiful flowing hair and my radiant beauty?"* He wrapped his dark cape around his face and shoulders to cover his shame. His eyes glowed over the top of its edges. *The Creator has done this!* He raised his fist to the heavens and cursed God *"**GOD WILL PAY!**"*

A Different Garden
Chapter Twenty-Eight

Adam rested against a boulder focusing on his and Eve's hunger.

He was oblivious to all things of the spirit. He was blind to Lucifer's machinations in the bowels of the earth, blind to God's interests on high, and blind to the two warrior angels standing nearby, guarding the entrance of the Garden of Eden where the Tree of Life grew.

All he knew, saw, and felt were his and Eve's hunger. His thoughts focused on the ache in his back as he tried, day after day, to gather enough food for both of them to survive. He rose with the sun and bedded down with the sun. Each morning the ritual would start again without gain. Sitting on a boulder exhausted, he watched Eve struggle to make a clearing for a garden. He wanted to help, but he had to focus on getting what they needed to sustain them daily. She cleared the weeds and was now turning the dark moist soil over, preparing it for seeds.

"I'm hungry," Eve complained. She tried to run her hand through her hair only to get her fingers caught in the dirty, tangled knots.

Adam laid his gatherings out before her on the ground and hung his head in failure. "Here are more greens, nuts, and berries. It is impossible to find enough to sustain us. The more we work, the hungrier we get." His cheek burned where a thorn had grabbed him.

"The garden is almost ready," Eve whimpered hopefully as she quickly ate the portions Adam offered. She was so tired she could hardly speak. "I just hope something grows before we starve." She looked at Adam's despondent face. "I'm sorry, Adam. This is my fault." She longed for the days of comfort they had known in Eden.

"No!" Adam insisted. "You were deceived but I knew what I was doing." Adam choked on his words, awash in guilt.

"If you knew what you were doing, then why did you take the fruit and eat it?" Eve asked, shocked at Adam's confession. "Why didn't you say 'no'?"

"I panicked. I knew if I chose to eat the fruit, I would lose the Creator, but if I didn't eat it, I would lose you." He reached out and pulled Eve close to him. He felt her tremble in the coolness of the setting sun. He also felt the softness of her face in his calloused hands. It pleased him to touch her. Sometimes he felt as though her beauty consumed him. She had become his entire world, and he had been willing to sin against God to keep her.

"When I tasted the fruit, nothing happened. So I didn't believe God...." Eve's words trailed off, her eyes growing heavy in sleepiness. "I wish I had understood. I mean really, really, understood. It tasted delicious so I thought it must be good for us."

"Just because something looks delicious doesn't mean it's good for us." Adam was silent. He realized that anything, no matter what it was, that caused him to sin was his idol.

"Yes," Eve gloomily agreed. "Listen to God ... not to me."

They paused in silence to hear the depth of their words amid the sounds of the forest: hooting, croaking, cooing, howling, and rustling.

"When God gives warnings, just because the consequences aren't immediate, does not mean God lied." Adam felt the warmth of his body close to Eve's skin. "But lessons won't save us now." Adam yawned.

The evening's sudden chill bit at them. They embraced each other in a feeble attempt to keep warm as the powerful, brilliant sun lowered behind and engulfed a spindly oak. Their skins of wool weren't keeping them warm. Together they crawled inside a dug out shelter Adam had fashioned in the side of a rocky cliff.

Sharing their skins of wool caused Eve to feel the pang of guilt. She remembered Seth, the little lamb which followed her everywhere in the Garden of Eden, leaping in playfulness, butting its head against her legs. Seth followed her into his own death as she and Adam looked for leaves to cover their nakedness. Seth was there when God interrupted them to ask what they had done. The fig leaves would not cover their sins, so God made them skins of wool, saying, "Without the shedding of blood, there is no forgiveness of sins." The memory haunted her. She would never forget her horror when she witnessed the life go out of Seth's eyes, his blood pooling on the earth. "I never want to see death again," Eve said, shuddering. "I wonder if that's what is going to happen to us."

"I don't think so," Adam said, trying to comfort her. "But I don't know." Adam did not want to tell her that he feared death just as much as she did. He had been wrestling with terrible nightmares. "We will wait for the prophesied One. He will crush the serpent's head, redeem us, and restore us to the Garden of Eden. There is hope, Eve."

"Yes," she said. "I forgot about God's promise." Eve snuggled close to her husband and sank into his arms. He made her feel safe.

Nothing Like This
Chapter Twenty-Nine

Close by, the angels Zuben and Menkib overheard everything.

"What do you think, Menkib?" Zuben asked.

"I don't know," Menkib answered. "How is one to make sense of this? The Creator made them with an ability to love each other with feelings we don't possess. When they embrace they radiate light around them in colors of soft hues. I have never seen anything like it among the angels. Have you?"

Zuben shook his head. "No, there's nothing like this among the angels in Heaven. They have dimensions of emotions we do not possess or understand – especially the woman."

"Is that good or bad?" Menkib asked.

"Always for good," Zuben replied. "Everything God does is for good ... somehow."

The Candidate
Chapter Thirty

In the war room buried within the cavern, Lucifer and Acamar (Lucifer's candidate for rebellion) sat facing one another on opposite sides of a table. Lucifer was ready to give Acamar an offer he couldn't refuse – blackmail.

The incandescent glow of a candle burning in the center of the table created two grotesque, enlarged shadows on the walls behind each one that loomed over their conversation.

On the fold-out desk of a curio cabinet set against the wall laid a contract waiting to be signed.

"Nothing you say will persuade me to rebel," Acamar began.

Lucifer smiled smugly. He knew Acamar would not be present, let alone engaged in a discussion, if there weren't something for him to gain.

Acamar shifted uncomfortably in his seat.

"Since there is nothing I can say," Lucifer said, leaning in, "then perhaps something I show you might cause you to reconsider." He rose and went to the cabinet and retrieved a key. "This is a copy of the key to the future worn by Auroran."

Acamar was aghast. "How did you get it?"

"From you," Lucifer countered. "Don't you remember? It is the key to the future you procured for me."

"But you were the administrator of Heaven then. You required it of me," Acamar said, defending his action. "I was obeying your authority." Acamar had never considered disobedience. He did not know how to respond.

"Why did you think I wanted you to hide your actions from Auroran?" Lucifer pressed. "Do you really think you are innocent? You deceive yourself, Acamar."

Acamar realized Lucifer had deceived him as he sat staring at the Archangel he had always admired. *Now the very sight of Lucifer disgusted him.* Acamar had never felt so confused.

"Nevertheless, the future confirms that I will win my war against the Almighty. I will be ruling the Heavens one day. And not I only, but any who follow me will rule with me." Then Lucifer fell silent. He wanted to give his guest time to comprehend what he was saying.

Acamar sat in stunned silence. After a considerable amount of time he spoke falteringly. "The future does not lie."

"You are right. And now this—" Lucifer pulled a scroll from his robe. He laid it in the hands of his naïve invitee to hold and to study.

Acamar read the title aloud: *The Pact of the Triune God*. "Is this what I think it is?" he asked.

"Only if you have concluded that it is God's plan for man. Look! Rolled up inside is the title deed giving man dominion over the earth."

"It's sealed with seven seals. You have no power to open it." Acamar was aghast.

"The holder of this mortgage has dominion over the earth, whether the seals are broken or not. Since I hold the mortgage deed, I am the dominator of the earth."

Acamar blinked. "What makes you believe God will allow you to keep the scroll or the deed? He will destroy you!"

"Will He?" Lucifer turned and smiled. "Can God suspend His *Laws of Righteousness* or the *Ordinances of Heaven?* Remember, God promised Adam and Eve a redeemer. If He were to destroy me, he would have to destroy his rebellious mankind. And if He were to destroy mankind, there would be no redeemer. That would make God a liar. If God lies, then that which binds the Heavens together will be loosed to the elements. No, the last state would be worse than the first."

Lucifer paused, observing Acamar's reaction closely. Then he continued. "God has no choice but to give me free reign without interference. God is in an untenable position. If God destroys mankind, He is a Liar and He has failed. Conversely, if God does not destroy mankind, then He is allowing disobedience – meaning, yet again, He has failed. Remember the first Law of Heaven? 'Those who contend with the Lord will be shattered.' Therefore, God has cornered Himself. He can neither destroy nor *not* destroy man. Either way He is no longer the righteous God whose throne is over the heavens and the earth. At some point He will have to step down."

Lucifer paused before adding: "At the next presentation of angels I intend to appear holding the Pact that contains the deed. I will declare myself to be the god of the earth. Then we will see if God is willing to sacrifice this mankind by destroying me. If not, then I will crown myself lord over all the earth in front of the hosts of angels, and then, upon crowning myself, I will have the authority to accuse men before the Divine Council in Heaven."

Acamar felt himself in the presence of a new kind of darkness – one he could not fathom nor, seemingly, resist.

"Let me show you that I am a generous leader," Lucifer said as he retrieved the document of rebellion from the desk of the curio cabinet. "I am offering you a position unlike any other: my chief advisor. Next to me, you will be the most powerful angel in my kingdom, the second in command. Has God offered you such a position?"

Acamar sat still, head lowered, thoughts paralyzed. "I cannot make this decision," he told Lucifer.

Lucifer straightened. "I will tell you what," Lucifer padded his offer. "The offer holds until the next presentation in Heaven. At the inception of the presentation I will appear and confront the Almighty. If He does not destroy me, then you will know I am correct. I only ask that you commit to leave with me if He does not destroy me to become my second in command. Conversely, if God *does* destroy me, then you have lost nothing and yet have everything to gain. Is that a deal?" Lucifer stood waiting. "But I will not hold your offer open beyond that. Surely there are others who would eagerly accept such an offer as this."

The heat in the smoldering room was intolerable. Acamar sweated profusely, rubbing his damp palms together.

Lucifer waited.

Acamar remembered how often in Heaven he had wanted to serve under Lucifer. How he desired just to catch Lucifer's attention. His face brightened. Acamar looked Lucifer full in the face and delivered his answer: "Deal."

"I must have your signature if I am to trust you will not change your mind." Lucifer scrawled the added terms and placed the document in front of Acamar.

Acamar hesitated.

Lucifer encouraged him: "If I am destroyed, this contract will be nothing to concern you."

Acamar took the pen and signed it.

Lucifer watched. Should Acamar change his mind at the presentation, Lucifer would declare that Acamar had taken the key from Auroran's belt and show everyone his signed document. *Acamar is mine!*

It *Is* True
Chapter Thirty-One

Borealis arrived in Ma'on after seeing Zuben and Menkib on earth. He went first to Auroran's house located just around the bend from the Honorarium. Farther on around the bend, Auroran's neighbor was the angel Wisdom whose house was built with the seven pillars of justice, truth, righteousness, honor, understanding, mercy, and servant-hood."

"Borealis! Where have you been?" Auroran gasped when he saw his brother. "You haven't seen Lucifer, have you? Have you heard?"

"So it *is* true," Borealis confirmed. "I found Zuben and Menkib guarding Eden. They told me Lucifer was in rebellion. I was hoping it wasn't true."

"I'm afraid so. The angel Gabriel is now the administrator of Heaven." Auroran groaned. He was happy to see his brother but grieved at the circumstances surrounding their reunion.

Each angel put his hand on the other's shoulder and lowered his head to acknowledge the gravity of the situation.

"Come," Auroran offered. "We can discuss the implications of these turn of events on the veranda." The veranda was Auroran's favorite place to enjoy the view of the valley. The portico floor was set in a soft blue tile that led to the edge of the cliffs. There, a brick-and-iron railing underlined the panoramic view before them.

Borealis walked through double doors into the temperate temperature and fresh air of the veranda. The bay window above jutted out from the house to served as an overhead porch. Outside, beside the doors, a trumpet vine extended from a tall planter up and around the side of the doors, through the banister of the large bay window overhead, and down the other side of the doors weaving itself along the brick-and-iron railing. Variegated purple trumpet flowers hung in clusters on the vine.

Auroran handed his brother refreshments. "I can't tell you how relieved I am to see you. Things are in such a mess." Auroran fell into a chair, exhausted. "I can't decide if the political imbroglio in the Heavens is over now that Lucifer has fallen or if the flaming winds of turmoil are just beginning to blow."

Auroran relaxed before confessing, "When you were absent, I thought Lucifer had recruited you."

"What? Who, me? Never!" Borealis crossed his brow. "You say Lucifer is recruiting angels? So who has joined him?"

Auroran sat up and leaned forward. "I don't know if any angel has joined him ... at least not yet, and I hope none does. But we shouldn't be naïve about his persuasive ways. You know his charisma. We shouldn't be caught unaware."

"Don't give it another thought," Borealis said, as he rose from his chair and looked away from the predominant worry-crease in his brother's forehead. "I have to go. I promised Zuben and Menkib I would return as soon as possible. One more thing: What is the news from the Throne Room?"

"Strangely enough, God is silent." Auroran trembled. He had an eerie sense, a void... it seemed as though God had allowed a distance, a gap to span between His presence and the angels. Again, he shivered. Were they being chastised? What could be happening...? None of the angels had ever experienced this "uneasiness" and no one could even speak of it ... for they didn't have the vocabulary and didn't know how. All he could do was relay the facts to his brother: "No information comes from the Temple – yet." Auroran wished God would call for an assembly of the angelic host and end the silence. Now, even he, Auroran, was asking many questions – even though he knew that they *must* trust God.

Brothers
Chapter Thirty-Two

Time on earth passed quickly for Zuben and Menkib, but not so quickly for Adam and Eve.

Eve rubbed her hands over her turgid, swollen stomach. It continued to swell with no end in sight. Her protruding stomach forced her backbone to bend backwards into an unnatural arc. Her breasts hurt. She believed this was death. The fear of death stalked her at every turn, lurked in every life-experience. For Eve, fear had become an invasive, exotic weed. It encroached upon her once lively personality and penetrated her soul. Fear was her constant companion. In the fullness of time she was shocked to see she had produced a child in the mist of blood and a placenta. During labor she believed she was experiencing death. It was not until after labor she began to understand this was to be a natural part of her life. Now she understood what God meant when He prescribed severe pain in childbirth as a curse for disobedience. Eve realized life could only come from life, while death could only produce death.

She gave birth to a daughter they named Beth. Adam delighted in the funny, little knot on the baby's tummy, since neither he nor Eve had one. It reminded Adam of the knot in the missing branch of the oak sapling.

Beth possessed her mother's beauty and her father's spirit. Filled with adventure, she was constantly looking beyond the fields wondering what lay beyond. Adam had wearied himself trying to convince her to stay behind with her mother. She wanted to go with him to the outer forest and beyond.

"Beth," Adam tried to explain, "Dangerous animals occupy the outer area." But she continued to run after him crying until, finally, Adam and Eve relented and let the child accompany him. After all, Eve reasoned, she now had her hands full with Beth's younger sisters, two of whom were still babies, and Beth wasn't a great deal of help.

In the glade, Adam allowed Beth to play at the boundaries of his vision, always watchful, always keeping an eye on her.

Zuben and Menkib enjoyed watching her as well, especially her constant exploring. Zuben found he could suggest ideas and she would hear them. He pointed out an interesting bird's nest that had fallen to the ground, some colored rocks, and a trickling waterfall her father did not know about.

By the time Beth had grown into a young lady, Eve gave birth to the first man child.

Adam was euphoric. When the child came forth, covered in blood, Adam performed his surgery. He cut the umbilical cord with his home made spear. Because of the cut, Eve named him "Spear" or "Cain."

After several more daughters, Eve then gave birth to another son. His birth, while painful, was relatively easy, so she named him "Whiff" or "Abel." Compared to Cain, Abel was a breeze. Furthermore; Cain had the birthright. Cain would be the one who would destroy the serpent and redeem them back into the Garden of Eden. So, while Abel was a male child, he wasn't as necessary as Cain. Just as a whiff or a breeze is nothingness and un-needed, so Abel was not really necessary.

Ideas
Chapter Thirty-Three

When the boys were babies, Beth continued to forage with her father. She became more adventurous and took risks Adam did not appreciate. But now that the boys were old enough to tag along, he could no longer focus on protecting her. While Adam focused on foraging for food and the boys played, Beth helped forage but also collected rocks and leaves that caught her interest. She used them for projects and decorations. She had no desire to help her mother with cooking, washing, or chores, but she proved to be a valuable help in foraging, in spite of her other activities.

Zuben watched Beth with a special interest. "She is delightful," he commented to Menkib.

"Don't forget the Forbidden Decree," Menkib reminded Zuben. "Angels are not to interbreed with the daughters of men. It is confusion."

"I've not forgotten," Zuben commented. "But I enjoy leaving items of joy for her to find."

Eve had many daughters. As they grew, they took to themselves their brothers. But Beth remained alone.

Adam's Gardener
Chapter Thirty-Four

Adam enjoyed teaching Cain; He was his little gardener. Abel however, turned away from gardening to herd sheep.

Cain derided herding sheep as a ridiculous waste of time. "What are you doing with all those sheep?" Cain asked.

"You will see," Abel replied.

The boys, their siblings, and Eve watched Adam's excitement as he exclaimed he had an idea for saving time in foraging.

"Why don't we find fruit and nut saplings, dig them up and plant them around the house? We won't have to go searching each and every day to find food. I know Cain is busy with the garden, but Abel can help. We'll have all the food we need right here around us," Adam smiled proudly.

The entire family celebrated his wonderful new vision, but when Abel heard his father's intentions, his face fell. His father did not understand how busy he had been with his own project. He wanted to surprise the family, but now he knew he would have to reveal what he was doing with the wool of his sheep.

Abel called together the members of his family for his own announcement. "Gather around," he said, as he retrieved wool from a bin. He showed them how he had cut the wool from his sheep, twisted the wool into threads, and made string. "See!" Abel announced. "You can shape it the way you want it. You can make it heavy or light."

"But, son," Adam argued, "you can cut a vine from one of the trees for string. Using wool isn't really necessary."

Adam corralled Abel into helping him with the orchard, but Abel could hardly wait to get back to working with wool.

As the boys grew older, they grew apart. Abel continued to be a keeper of sheep, but Cain was a tiller of the ground. Abel had discovered how to make blankets and weave patterns into his blankets even though his father didn't see the necessity of blankets either.

"Get those filthy sheep out of my garden!" Cain screamed at his brother, furious that one of Abel's sheep was destroying his harvest.

"I can't help where the sheep wander." Abel tried to reason with his brother. "I try my best to keep them away."

"This garden is our food! Without it, we will starve. Don't you understand that includes *you?*" Cain fumed. "While you mess around with sheep, I have to do all the work. You and your blankets won't feed us!" Frustrated, Cain tried to rehabilitate some of the plants one of the sheep had trampled.

"I'll fix that," Abel said, throwing himself into his brother's work. "Why don't we put some of this string up around the garden to protect it?"

"Never mind. Just get those sheep out of here. They're not good for anything," Cain grumbled as he replanted the vegetables that had been pulled up. *Life was hard enough without destroying what had already been done.*

"I'm sorry, Cain," Abel said. "I really am. Let me help." Abel got his ball of string to prop and tie a semi-broken vegetable vine.

"You know the harvest feast is coming. You know how we were planning a banquet, and these beautiful onions ... look at them ... these I wanted to sacrifice to the LORD." Cain was distraught.

"But Cain...." Abel blinked as he thought about how to respond to his hot-headed brother. "We've been told to sacrifice a lamb, one without blemish."

"That's it! I've had it!" Cain lost all control. "**You!** Because of you Dad isn't working this garden like he should. He's obsessed with his orchard and on top of that he's helping you instead of me. It's up to me to take care of this entire household. **You** should be gardening! Why should I have to take care of **you?** Why should I be your keeper?"

Abel backed off, realizing it was better to leave his brother to himself. As he looked back, he hoped Cain would see how well the string was working. If he saw it, he might change his mind.

Zuben and Menkib were nearby, guarding the entrance to the Garden of Eden. They were exhausted listening to Cain's tirades. His anger radiated in yellows, oranges, and reds.

Adam's Greatest Fear
Chapter Thirty-Five

"What's Cain fighting about now?" Menkib asked wearily.

"Cain wants to sacrifice vegetables to God," Zuben explained. "But Abel insists on sacrificing a lamb just as God instructed."

"Cain is right in one sense," Menkib offered. "It makes no sense to spill blood."

"But God's instructions must be followed," Zuben replied. "He has a reason for every instruction, even when it doesn't follow logic. Think back. God covered Adam and Eve's sin by removing their fig leaves and replacing them with the skin of a slain lamb. Now, God is requiring a slain lamb to cover their daily sins. Like the fig leaves, vegetation is not an option. Without the shedding of blood, there is no covering for sin."

"Of course, obedience," Menkib said. He paused before adding, "Men can no longer easily relate to obedience. He has no sense of trusting. He only does that which he desires for himself."

"With exceptions," Zuben interjected, pointing toward Abel.

"Yes, with exceptions," Menkib agreed. "But in Cain, troubles do not end; they multiply continually. Each day brings more fighting and more bickering."

"That is the result of sin," Zuben offered, "a spiritual disease with an unnatural bent to transgress God's laws."

"Adam becomes angry with Eve and Eve manipulates Adam, which makes Adam even angrier. And so on and on." Menkib was weary of men. *It was an endless cycle.*

Zuben reminded Menkib: "Didn't God say Eve's desire would be for her husband? They both seek their own interests, which makes them both predators. But since Eve is the weakest physically, and the most vulnerable, she has to rely on her husband for protection."

"But her husband's anger makes *him* the predator. How can *he* protect her? Haven't you noticed how self-centered Adam has become?" Menkib wrinkled his nose. The smell of sin was pervasive. The stench had become impossible to ignore. "It seems to me Eve's greatest protector is also her worst enemy. He hits her when he becomes angry."

"She has to keep him pleased. Unfortunately, the only way she can get what she needs or wants is to manipulate him. Both are trying desperately to retain their dignity and value. Adam's greatest fear is that Eve will laugh at him, while Eve's greatest fear is that Adam will kill her."

Zuben and Menkib pondered their insights. They noticed Adam and Eve couldn't live without a sense of community so they stayed together – even in the worst of fights.

"Angels can survive alone, but men need companionship," Zuben added. He had made a study of them. *They were a passionate creation, with emotions deeper than any angel could endure. Angels had concerns, cares, and feelings they used in their service to God, but they did not emotionally connect in the ways men did. Since the souls of men were soft opalescent bubbles that clung to each other sharing a common membrane, they were incapable of detaching without great suffering. Any detachment left the membrane mutilated and disfigured.*

"Man is not the only oddity in this aberrant universe." Menkib offered. "Have you noticed how - when we angels fold ourselves into man's four dimensions to be seen by men, they can't see our wings, yet we can see our own wings."

It was an anomaly that neither Zuben nor Menkib could explain.

- - - - -

Lucifer's stomach clawed at him. Never before had he felt hunger. Clutching himself, he watched Adam sitting alone, content. *This should not be; he was in misery and Adam was content.*

Lucifer saw Adam radiating in soft hues.

He wanted to claw Adam and tear him apart. He approached Adam and discovered his emotional hue was touchable. He tore at a piece of Adam's emotions. He was so hungry he would eat anything. It was bland, but it filled his stomach. He chewed on it and swallowed just to relieve the emptiness.

As Lucifer tore at Adam's hue, Adam felt something uncomfortable deep inside his soul.

Adam's emotions changed and he became agitated, unaware Lucifer tore at him, eating away his hue.

Lucifer noticed Adam's hue changed from blue to orange. Lucifer spewed the blue hue from his mouth in order to taste the orange hue. He discovered the orange had a more satisfying flavor. Lucifer soon learned Adam's blazing red emotions of fear and anger tasted best.

With this realization, Lucifer quickly began whispering lie upon lie into Adam's ear to produce fear and anger. Lucifer reminded Adam of every mistake he had made, every child who had done him wrong, how Eve tempted him in the Garden, and how naïve he had been. The angrier Adam became, the more Lucifer gorged himself until liquid red trickled from the corners of his mouth.

Lucifer learned shame and guilt produced anger while twisted thought patterns produced fear. He knew he had found a supply of food, enough to feed all the angels who wished to rebel. He realized that from man's hue, there was enough light for a fallen angel to survive, but he was, as yet, unaware each bite lessened man's life span.

Talk Business
Chapter Thirty-Six

Etán was bored shoveling hailstones. He wasn't restless, but he wasn't motivated either. He had never been promoted or earned a medallion at an assembly of promotions. Immediately following each assembly he would work hard, but his motivation never lasted. He would ultimately fall back into mindless, repetitive motions. He decided to seek out another assignment, but he asked himself: *Where do I look? How do I start?* Even that determination diminished and he reveled in his lack of responsibility.

Today, as he left his assignment, he loosed his hair that he had pulled back behind his neck to contain it. He felt like exploring. He chose to take a different path than normal. He wondered why he had not tried this path before, or even noticed it. He couldn't decide whether to fly or just walk in order to save his angelic energy, so he walked. He saw and noticed many things he had never seen before. He also heard angels talking alongside the roadway. He was surprised to think other angels were in this seemingly forgotten area of heaven. He couldn't contain his amazement to see Lucifer and Acamar in a deep conversation alongside the roadway. *What was Lucifer doing on the Isle of Makon? What was Acamar doing with Lucifer? What were they doing on this forgotten, isolated path? Hadn't Lucifer rebelled? Evidently this information was not truth.* He was equally taken aback when the two angels approached him.

"Etán!" Lucifer greeted him.

"Ho," Etán replied in a state of wonderment. *Why would Lucifer be greeting him in such an amiable manner?*

Lucifer gave Etán a hardy welcome. "Look at this angel's strength." Lucifer complimented him to Acamar.

Etán glowed. His strength was his dignity.

"It is a shame he uses it for nothing more than shoveling in the warehouse," Acamar added.

"I'm surprised he hasn't been promoted," Lucifer paused to consider his words, "to a position worthy of his strength."

"I've been looking for another position," Etán confessed.

"Have you?" Lucifer looked surprised. "I may have something to offer you."

Etán was captivated when Lucifer suggested they talk business.

A Tarnished Crown
Chapter Thirty-Seven

"Come and Hear!" The Archangel blew his trumpet. The sound drew the attention of every angel in the vicinity. He blew his trumpet a second time, then lifted the announcement and read: "Gabriel, the new administrator of Heaven calls for a roll call to be held. All angels must present themselves before the Lord God Almighty. Absent angels will be listed as fallen." The Archangel provided the meeting details of how and where before he flew off to repeat the announcement in other vicinities.

On the day of the roll call, Zuben and Menkib were temporarily relieved of their duties. Auroran, D'shubba, Zuben, Menkib, Wisdom, Borealis, and Choices went as a group into the assembly hall.

As they waited among the myriads of angels in a crowded hall, a flaming ball of fire jetted over their heads before crashing in front of the Veil of the Lord.

This flash of fire caused angels to fall back in shock and awe.

The fireball broke apart, revealing Lucifer.

When Zuben realized it was Lucifer he charged, grabbing him around his chest. Borealis likewise pulled Lucifer down from behind even as Menkib and other angels followed Zuben's lead.

A chaotic disruption ensued in the hall.

Just as they were about to bring Lucifer under total subjugation and arrest him, the Hand of God, like a Dove, quietly lit on Zuben's fist. When

Zuben saw this, he released Lucifer. Other angels followed suit, loosing their grip one by one.

Hosts of angels watched in awe.

Lucifer, pulling himself loose and gathering his sense of decorum, stepped up to make his declaration. "I, Lucifer, now hold the title deed to the dominion of the earth. According to the Laws of Heaven, this gives me the right to be god of the earth and the lord over mankind." Lucifer waved the unopened scroll over his head for every angel to witness. "I stand here today to crown myself and receive my inheritance." Lucifer turned toward the Veil. "Strike me down or give me my inheritance. If You destroy me, however, You must also destroy mankind who has likewise rebelled, as instituted under the Laws and Ordinances of Heaven."

Lucifer lifted his crown and was about to position it on his head when a thunderbolt struck it from his hands and sent it rolling into the audience of angels.

The voice of God thundered from behind the Veil, echoing from mountaintop to mountaintop. "Of man's world, you are ruler; of men, you are not. He who follows you will follow you, but he who does not follow you, is not yours. If free will is taken from man, then it will be taken also from you."

The angels bowed low as God spoke to Lucifer, the accuser of God and men.

"Of the earth only, take possession. You are no longer Lucifer the bearer of Light, but in disgrace you are 'Ha Satán,' The Accuser. He who accuses is destined to be clothed with disgrace and cloaked in shame, but the crown on my Anointed will shine."

The angels gawked at Ha (the) Satán (Accuser) who lost his crown when God struck it with a thunderbolt and sent it rolling, the Satán who was forced to bow low when he humiliatingly had to chase his tarnished crown as it rolled among the hosts of angels.

Upon retrieving his crown, Satán stood to crown himself once again. Turning toward the assembly of angels he urged them to rebel, "Take charge! Exercise your option of free will. Show your strength." Lucifer then disappeared as he had arrived, in a flash of fire taking Acamar with him, forcing Acamar to show his shame.

"What should we make of this?" Auroran whispered.

"I think that is his fate," D'shubba commented, "he will perish as he arrived, in a ball of fire."

"Acamar was taken!" various angels exclaimed. "Did he rebel?" The question passed through the rows of angels creating a wave undulating across the oceans of angels.

Zuben and Menkib returned to their duties in the Garden of Eden. They found scorching imprints where their feet had left a permanent scar in the earth over the earth years. They were worn thin with this assignment and passed their time discussing Satán as they again produced flaming swords to guard the entrance to the Garden of Eden. The roll call had been a welcome break from their relentless duty, but now they wondered if the tedious assignment would ever end.

The only break for Zuben was his interest in Beth. He was constantly on the look for her and ever thinking about unexpected gifts to leave for her. He loved to hear her laugh, her way with the animals of the forest, and watch as she made funny, little things that gave her pleasure. He felt ever increasingly protective of her and from time to time he desired to leave his post to find her, but pushed those desires aside to continue his assignment.

"Why do you think it is that God continues to have us here?" Menkib asked. "Why doesn't He simply remove the Tree of Life so men won't have access to it?"

Zuben thought about it. He didn't have an answer.

"Do you think God has forgotten about us being here?" Menkib couldn't help but ask.

Zuben laughed. "No, I'm sure God does not have a short memory. There must be a reason."

As Zuben and Menkib guarded the entrance to the Garden of Eden, Satán indulged himself in his "free will" deep within the bowels of the earth.

Encapsulated in darkness, Satán resided as an unholy fetus in the womb of mother earth. He no longer reported to God. He now had authority to accuse men before God in God's own Heaven. His accusations gave him the right to punish men if his arguments held true before the Divine Counsel.

Every move Satán made against the God of the Heavens proved futile, for God used it to turn the tables on Satán.

A Needed Rest
Chapter Thirty-Eight

Men, according to their sin nature, tended to grow toward evil and away from God, especially when they prospered.

Only when reaching a critical level of despair would men then call out to God. The God of the broken hearted waited until he was called upon before he would cool a man's hurting heart; for men had free will to accept God or reject God.

Pain, then, served as the thermostat of heat working against sin. When men felt the heat, they saw the Light. Pain became a teacher of reality and compassion; for only in obedience to God and servitude to men, could a man find his rest.

This was something Satán could never understand.

- - - - - -

How strange, Satán grumbled. *I am exhausted, but I cannot sleep. I work, but I cannot rest.* He reached upward as he had always done in order to enter into his rest – but nothing happened. His form remained intact. With intensity he concentrated again as hard as he could, almost straining. Finally, after much time, something let loose. He felt himself go, but before losing consciousness he realized he had not much light left; God must have been his only source of light. He didn't know what he would do when his light was completely extinguished. Even eating the hue of men could not supply enough light to provide rest. This may, he thought, be his last rest.

Beneath the dark caverns, deep in the recesses of the earth, amid the stagnant dripping stalactites, Satán slept while Acamar worked. Above, on the face of the earth, an unexplained calmness came over Cain as his turbulence was temporarily stilled.

When Satán woke he was famished. In heaven, he never knew hunger or neediness. Now, each time he ate, he needed more. His appetite became insatiable; his addiction consumed him. He had to find a man to agitate in order to eat. Upon finding Cain, he whispered in his ear accusations against his brother, Abel. As Satán feasted, he whispered, "murder, murder, murder," and as he did, Cain became angrier and angrier.

The Hierarchy
Chapter Thirty-Nine

The first meeting of Satán's hierarchy began. Four angels, in addition to Acamar, had rebelled.

Maps, hung haphazardly, covered the walls of the war room. The rebels sat around an uneven table in the center of the room. A knurled, locked curio cabinet protecting an array of gothic objects leaned against the yellowed wall.

Satán spoke. "Acamar is second only to me. His name is no longer Acamar, but Akkamar." Satán pointed to his "Second" among the seated rebels, "Please introduce yourself Akkamar."

Akkamar took his place at the head of the table. "You knew me as Acamar in the third heaven. I abandoned my position as one of the unknown and invisible stars. I did so in accordance with my will as a free agent. By serving Satán, I am the angel of chaos. I sit in the council of the unconstrained. You four, as well as myself, will be the hierarchy of fallen angels. To my left is Kasdaye, the angel of satanic practices. Stand, please, Kasdaye."

Kasdaye stood, his slouched hat cocked to one side on his head. His goatee twisted on his chin as he smiled. He waved his hand in the air painting pictures in a trail of sparkles and smoke. Finished, he sat again, saying not a word.

"Kasdaye is our magician," Akkamar noted. "Next to Kasdaye sits Lyrid Mot, the angel of sickness, famine, disease, and death."

All eyes focused on an emaciated, weak-shouldered, chinless angel clad in an oversized robe with a hood hung over his head.

Akkamar continued. "Lyrid Mot is called the angel of misery. Lyrid's presence is *infectious*," Akkamar quipped, pleased with his clever pun.

Lyrid Mot took his turn of acknowledgement, coughing and wheezing as he stood.

The group stared at this listless angel —small, unassuming, and withered. His clothes hung from the small protrusions of his body. What could this angel possibly have to offer?

"Next to Lyrid Mot is Etán."

The group turned their eyes to a muscular, bulked-up figure resembling a hulk dressed in chlorophyll-green garments. The contrast between Lyrid Mot and Etán could not be more vivid.

"Etán is the angel of war, violence, and murder," Akkamar explained.

Etán stood slowly. His low-set brows and angry eyes confronted everyone at the table. He rolled his shoulders forward. When no one challenged him, he sat down.

"Thank you, Etán," Akkamar said. "Lastly, I present Marcus, the angel of unnatural pleasures and addictions."

Marcus exuded charm and charisma. His wavy black hair framed his handsome face as he stood and bowed. His skill was to get others to do whatever he wanted. His clothes were exquisitely fitted and immaculate.

Marcus was the last of the new rebels.

Akkamar then pointed to Satán who stood nearby, leaning against the strange curio cabinet. All eyes looked his way. "Satán, the sixth, our leader, represents us all," Akkamar concluded. "He is the angel of deception, betrayal, and lies." Akkamar then took his seat.

Satán nodded in acknowledgment. He opened a small drawer in the curio cabinet and removed a handful of pocket-sized objects. Without a word, he walked around the table, handing each angel a compass bearing no direction markers. "These compasses of truth are broken. At one time they pointed to *True North*, but notice how they now spin without direction. These are your weapons against mankind. The more man uses your special compass, the more lost he will become. I am here to aid in your pursuit of the captivity of men. As you know, you have unquestioned authority when it comes to bringing man into subjugation. He is yours for enslavement, serfage, bondage, confinement, duress, and imprisonment. You may use torture, abuse, brutality, calamity, coercion, torment, suffering, pleasure, or tyranny to achieve your goals. In short, man is yours for the taking. Do with them as you please. Take from man what you will, but pay me my due homage."

"What of Zuben and Menkib?" The broad-faced Etán asked. "Will they try to interfere?"

"You are now princes!" Satán shot back. "Build your kingdoms! Fight as needed, be clever; use your resources. How can you succeed unless you are willing to reach out and take that which is yours?"

After Satán adjourned the meeting, the rebel angels disbanded to claim their respective territories using their unique *gifts*.

Archways with heavy wooden doors and iron latches served as the gatekeepers of private trysts, secret glances, and whispered conversations.

East of Eden
Chapter Forty

Beth, now fully a woman, was alone. With no brothers for her to marry, she continued her explorations at every opportunity. At home contentions and squabbling grew. She couldn't wait to escape the melee between the families. She sought out the peaceful serenity of the forest. She wanted a life of her own but remained inexorably bound to her family. Her sisters had mates, but she remained alone.

She shook her frustration aside, choosing to focus on the beauty of the day. A strange new fruit bulging with nectar hung from a low-hanging vine beside her. The vine had coiled itself around a tree trunk. Beth reached up and touched the fruit that was exposed to the heat of the sun. It had split, its nectar dripping into the earth.

Beth plucked the fruit from the vine. She sat on a fallen tree trunk and took a bite of it. She felt inspired to compose a song in her head. She thought about the stories her father and mother had shared and their love for each other in Eden. She was a romantic who wove words and music together into verbal garlands:

> "On naked trees and limbs there grew, a budding love that we but knew ... in Eden.
>
> With warnings of a future fall, ignoring all, we broke God's law ... in Eden.
>
> Turgid fruits hang low on vines to swell and part and intertwine ... in Eden.
>
> Passion pulsing like the sun, two beating hearts melt into one ... in Eden."

Beth stopped, remembering her parents' stories of that fateful day and how they had been thrown out of Eden. Then she continued:

> "What our sin and what our crime to toss us out and leave behind ... our Eden?

Must love but bloom upon the vine, to wither up and curl, and die … in Eden?"

Beth looked thoughtfully into the future, trying to see what might lie ahead as she wove word upon word.

"Time drifts, and drifts, eternally, waiting for its pain to heal … in Eden.

Frozen pain, like ice will melt. Forgiveness then, will soon be felt: in Eden."

Beth was enamored with thoughts of love as she sat alone, humming her lilting tune to the words she had constructed, unaware of the sinister figure near her.

Marcus
Chapter Forty-One

Beth could not see Marcus.

His every muscle tensed as he was ready to reveal himself to Beth in her dimension – when suddenly he was interrupted.

"Marcus!" Zuben shouted.

Startled, Marcus looked up to see Zuben coming toward him. His lips curled into a snarl. "What is this to you, Zuben?"

Zuben chastised him. "You know the Forbidden Decree given at Creation."

"Ha!" Marcus laughed. "What is that to me? Have you forgotten you are under God's laws while I am not?"

"You will not plague her," Zuben pushed.

Marcus and Zuben circled each other.

"I relinquished my position in my first domain in order to have free will," Marcus answered. "Do you really think I will stand down to you?"

Zuben moaned inwardly. What Marcus had said was true, and he was powerless to stop him. His only option was to rebuke him in the name of the Lord.

Marcus laughed and flew off while Zuben was forced to return to his post.

When Zuben returned some time later, Menkib asked, "What is it? You are flushed."

"I am beginning to understand the implications of sin," Zuben replied. "It's going to become more and more difficult to comply with God's directives as men multiply."

Marcus circled back on Beth after Zuben returned to his post. She was still composing and singing when he folded himself into her dimension.

Alarmed, Beth looked up to see a handsome giant of a man standing in front of her. She almost fell off of the round bench. "Who are you?" she chirped.

"I heard your singing," Marcus smiled. "I was beguiled by your voice."

Nod
Chapter Forty-Two

Marcus was the first of the hierarchy to take a woman, laying claim to Beth. He found her quite beautiful. He courted her with charm and charisma and she, being enamored, fell easily for his persuasions. He had managed to seduce her into his unholy power.

Together, they grew a family of giants east of Eden, in Nod.

The rest of the hierarchy followed suit. As many as they could charm, they took. Children were born to these unions. They became the mighty men of legend, giants who populated the earth, and were worshiped as gods by mortal men. But they originated in Nod.

The Attic
Chapter Forty-Three

Satán used his access to the thirteenth dimension of man's rest to explore the attic of Adam's mind. He brought his bag of seedy lies. As he pulled at gossamer webs of Adam's memories, they came alive. In the dust-filled room, disconnected memories played out in holographic images then quickly faded away.

Satán choked on the dust. He was claustrophobic under the low rafters. This dimension was unpredictable and chaotic. It might have been worth it if he were able to read Adam's thoughts. He was sorely disappointed to discover he could not.

He opened a trunk to find it filled with rotting guilt and shame. He shut the lid quickly. He now lost his curiosity and wanted to finish the job he had come to do. Dragging his bag of seedy lies across the dusty floor, he scattered them randomly about the room.

The dark attic unexpectedly lit up. Satán felt a shock.

The onslaught of lies had set off a panic attack in Adam. Lightning flashed in the window to Adam's thought processes, which were clashing with his emotions.

Thunder exploded while bolts of lightning flashed veins of light revealing horror upon horror. Lucifer crawled under a supporting beam, forced to ride out the storm until he could escape.

- - - - -

When Adam woke he shivered in his sweat.

He was like Beth, or Beth was like him. They were poets who expressed themselves in writing. After his night of terror, Adam documented his experience in poetry:

> Black, the darkness, Deep, the night.
> Inward - Outward – Gusts of fright.
>
> Cobwebs cloud the cluttered mind,
> Where something evil leaves behind
> Memratic bits of every kind.
>
> Thunder! Lightning! Sheets of pain.
> A face that flashes... fades again.
>
> Tears seep through walls that can't contain
> the mask of rage that drives insane.
>
> Is there a room to hold this sadness?
> Which door...or knob...that leads to madness?
>
> Tormented beings come and go,
> While nightmares toss me to and fro.
>
> Candles wane. Thoughts are frantic!
> Surging terror, states of panic.
>
> Black the future. Deep the fright.
> Forever waiting – for the Light.

The Attic.

Following his nightmarish attack, Adam began a process of building thought patterns to help him keep mentally stable. He decided God had to be in control of his life, to believe things would get better – not worse, that he had value and was loved. After all, "right now" was all that mattered. He chose not to look at their future since their future looked hopeless.

Adam gave his heart and soul to God for safekeeping.

Tables Turned
Chapter Forty-Four

From His throne in the seventh Heaven, from Araboth, God's eyes pierced Satán's cavern. God foreknew each move Satán made as he promoted his evil rebellion, and used it to turn the tables on Satán, promoting the kingdom of righteousness in its stead. Satán was oblivious to God's oversight.

On this occasion, God flooded Adam's attic with Holy Light. When Light invades darkness, the darkness has no choice but to cower and hide behind objects as nothing more than mere shadows, full of fear and threats – menacing, but empty of substance.

The Pit
Chapter Forty-Five

"We are alone Borealis," Satán assured him. "God cannot see you here."

Borealis had contacted Satán to negotiate a position of rebellion in his kingdom.

Satán leaned back and sized up Borealis who was sitting across from him. *Borealis has a higher status in Heaven than any previous angel who had rebelled, and his brother was no other than the angel Auroran.* Satán could hardly keep his composure. "What is it that causes you to want to rebel?" Satán asked.

"I'm tired of God's assignments," Borealis replied as he felt the suffocating darkness of Satán's cavern bear down on him. He looked around and over his shoulder as he continued. "I want to be free to do as I wish." Borealis made mental notes on every aspect of Satán's territory. "If I join you," Borealis said, getting to the point, "I want be the second in command under you."

"That position," Satán paused, "has been given to Akkamar. You already knew that Borealis – so why would you ask such a thing?"

"I have a bargaining chip," Borealis said, smiling. "Unbeknownst to Auroran I made a copy of his key to the bottomless pit. Has Akkamar been so valuable?"

Satán politely offered Borealis an extract of potion for a drink. "If I wanted such a key, I would have made a copy myself before I left my first station." Satán took his time as he strode behind Borealis.

"But you did not." Borealis smiled as he sipped from the cup set before him.

"You are unaware, Borealis, that in this kingdom we all pitch in for the good of everyone. If you have such a key, I would think you would wish to donate it regardless of the position you were offered. You would not expect me to break a promise to Akkamar would you?"

"I apologize, *Sir Satán*." Borealis smirked. "I was under the impression that you were in charge and able to make your own decisions. I was wrong in believing you were able to do as you wish. Now I see my error. I retract my ignoble offer. Again, forgive me; I thought you were in charge. I will leave you in peace."

"Peace?" Satán rankled, "What peace is there since God created this war?" Satán charged head on. "What has **He** done to prevent this violence? Nothing, I tell you. By now He should have stepped down."

As Satán pontificated, Borealis listened in astonishment at Satán's twisted logic.

"It's time for me to leave." Borealis rose.

"You will **not** leave." Satán's viciousness emerged. He leaned into Borealis' face, nose to nose. "Have you considered this: No one in Heaven knows you're here. You would never tell them you were coming to rebel. Therefore, there is none to save you. I can do anything with you I wish. I did not trust you when you wanted to meet with me and I do not trust you now." Satán called his rebels. "Etán! Kasdaye!"

Two angels rushed in, shocked to find Borealis in the war room with Satán.

"Shake him down," Satán hissed. "He has a copy of the key to the bottomless pit and I wager he has it on him!"

The two angels pounced on him, wrestling with him as they held him down until they could reach into his pocket sash where they recovered a large, heavy black key.

"Behold the irony." Satán laughed, standing over Borealis with his key. "Lock him up." Satán stepped on Borealis' neck. "I never took you for being so naïve, Borealis." Satán turned his attention to Etán and Kasdaye who were holding Borealis face down. "We now have a hostage. Here is the key to his imprisonment which he, himself, delivered. How thoughtful of you, Borealis."

Etán and Kasdaye proceeded to drag Borealis away.

"Careful you don't get too close!" Satán yelled after the rebels. "Or the pit will suck you in. Toss him in from a distance!"

Borealis struggled and fought, but a horde of fallen angels gathered as he was being dragged away, each one lending their strength to constrain him. A strange sleepiness came upon him. He suspected Satán of spiking the potion, and realized he was literally being "drug" away.

Unable to act as one, the band tugged and pulled until the rebels finally succeeded in throwing Borealis into the pit.

A Different Substitute
Chapter Forty-Six

Menkib and Zuben froze. They stared at each other when they heard a terrible shriek, each looking for a quick answer in the face of the other.

"What was that?" A wide-eyed Zuben asked.

"I don't know!" Menkib replied, dazed.

The shrieking and wailing continued until finally Zuben told Menkib, "I can't stand it any longer. Menkib, *please go* and see what it is!"

"I can't abandon my post!" Menkib protested.

"You won't. I'll cover for both of us...." Zuben grabbed Menkib's sword in one adept swipe. He held one flaming sword in his left hand and one flaming sword in his right hand, the swords turning in sync. "Go quickly!" he shouted as the screams continued.

Menkib found the source of the undiminished piercing wails. He found Eve, crumpled on the ground, shrieking in despair. He looked up as he heard another voice from afar.

"Eve! What is it?"

Menkib saw Adam running toward her from across the field. The animals peered from behind trees and bushes around the glade. Menkib had reached Eve before Adam but was forced to stand by, helpless. To equip himself to help her he would have had to fold himself into four dimensions. He had no such authority. Furthermore, he was unable to ascertain what was amiss, but the light around her was dark, if such a thing could be. He stood by waiting.

When Adam reached Eve, she looked up at him with her distorted face and wailed. She was clutching something muddy, something large and heavy that she held against her breast. Adam tried to wrap his arms around her, to pick her up, to carry her, but she would not let go. Blood had clotted and mixed with dirt, creating a strange red mud that covered the object and caused the dirt to stick to the front of her clothing. He tried to identify what Eve clung to so desperately. As he pulled on her, to separate her from her burden, a pained recognition crept across his face. Adam froze. He let go of Eve. In shock he fell backward and sat on the ground staring at his own mud-encrusted, blood-soaked hands. "Abel is ... dead...?" Adam looked again. His son's head had been bashed in. He looked around, dazed. "Where's Cain?"

Menkib looked up scanning the field for any sight of Cain. He saw Cain hiding with a rock in his hand and blood on his clothes. But another stood by. Menkib saw Etán standing over Cain, grinning. Sickened, Menkib said nothing to the hulk-like darkened angel but rushed back to the Garden's entrance. Like Eve, *he* wanted to cry out ... to scream. *Etán had rebelled! How many other angels had followed Satán? Is this what life and death will be like for mankind in the ages to come?* He retched involuntarily.

"What is it, Menkib?" Zuben demanded. *"What's wrong?"*

Menkib couldn't talk; he took both swords from Zuben. "Go and see for yourself, Zuben.... I will hold the swords." When Zuben left, Menkib knew he had made a decision: *I need a replacement for this assignment as soon as possible!*

Not His Keeper
Chapter Forty-Seven

The angels in the arena peered intently into Corona as God confronted Cain about his brother. They fell back hearing his irreverent answer. "How should I know where Abel is? I'm not his keeper, am I?"

The warrior, Perseus, who was Menkib's replacement at the temple doors, was startled. "He shows neither reverence nor regret."

As God pronounced sentence over Cain, for him the earth would no longer give its strength to his hand, those from the court of the Divine Council agreed this was just and right.

The angels clamored: "How will he eat?" "What will he do?" "Must he die?"

"He ran to Nod. Perhaps his sisters' families will share their food," one angel speculated.

"No," another shot back. "They will kill him. He will be a burden, an unwanted guest."

"My punishment *is* greater than I can bear!" Cain wept. "You are driving me out from the face of the ground; I shall be hidden from your face. Who will take a fugitive and a vagabond? Anyone who finds me will kill me."

God had compassion and engraved the letter Zayin, representing a sword, in Cain's forehead with His finger. It was a warning to others not to commit the same offense knowing if they did they would incur God's wrath seven times over. It reminded all who saw Cain that God is a returning light of judgment and the sustenance of men.

Perseus marveled. *Would anyone dare kill Cain?*

Perseus and Pyro
Chapter Forty-Eight

Perseus was relieved as a temple assignment to be given an assignment with Pyro, the angel of fire. They reported immediately and were assigned to gather as much information as possible on the rebel angels. Furthermore, they were directed to remove the Tree of Life from the Garden of Eden and return it to Heaven. Evidently, there was evidence Satán had planned to get the tree and use it for his own purposes. They were instructed not to discuss the second directive concerning the Tree of Life.

"Your points of contact are Zuben and Menkib," the directive insisted.

"If we are going to earth," Perseus said, "I wish we were making the trip with Borealis."

Pyro shared in this desire, but no one had seen Borealis, which was not unusual.

Their first trip to earth was intriguing. Upon locating the Garden of Eden with Zuben and Menkib, greetings were made all around. Pyro explained their assignment on collecting information about the rebels.

"If you are going to stake out the area," Menkib cautioned, "be careful not to be seen. Be wary. It is easy to find yourself trapped."

"Stay away from Nod," Zuben cautioned. "And stay away from the daughters of men. It's easy to become involved with them. We are commanded not to interfere."

"Where is Nod?" Perseus wanted to know.

"It is east of here. Also, Satán's cavern is deep in the earth," Menkib pointed to one of many entrances. "The entrances in our dimensions are many and varied."

"We're only going to work on the face of the earth," Pyro updated them. He then asked the guardians about the offensive smell.

"It's something you will have to get used to," Zuben answered without encouragement.

Cain's Birthright
Chapter Forty-Nine

Eve's days of weeping were endless. She used to tell her children how one day, one of Cain's sons would destroy the power of the serpent and redeem them so they could return to the Garden of Eden. She took pleasure in repeating the promises God had made. She also described the Tree of Life and how they ate from it and never aged.

"What was *that* like?" The older ones always urged her to tell them more.

"There was neither death nor fear," she would affirm, smiling.

"No death?" they exclaimed.

"No death," she would repeat.

Each time she told her stories she made sure to reiterate the importance of sacrificing as the LORD specified. "You see, fig leaves could not cover our sin. It had to be the spilling of blood. Without the spilling of blood, there is no forgiveness of sins."

She reminisced. She remembered her dismay when she saw the look of her own disobedience mirrored in the face of her first son, Cain.

He had disobeyed even as she had disobeyed.

Now, it didn't matter. Her second son, Abel, was dead, killed by Cain, the holder of the family's birthright. She wept endlessly. When Cain killed Abel, he not only sacrificed his birthright but the ability to produce a redeemer. For the first time it dawned on her that she would not live to see their return to Eden.

Adam, however, became more determined not to succumb to unending grief. When Eve once again became pregnant, when she gave birth to a third male child on a beautiful spring day, they both agreed the days ahead would be better.

"What shall we call him?" she whispered as she laid her new son on her breast.

"Substitute," Adam answered. "The promise of a redeemer will come through this substitute," and so, like the lamb, they named him "Seth."

"Seth is a substitute for Cain even as the lamb was a substitute clothing our sins." Eve commented to her husband.

"Yes," Adam answered, "but this substitute will save us in a different way. Through his seed, his descendents, the redeemer will surely come. He now has Cain's birthright."

The Daughter of a Man
Chapter Fifty

Perseus cautiously surveyed an area thought to be safe. All he saw were grapes hanging from vines. *As long as I am here, why not try man's food?* He secretly changed into man's dimensions in order to experience this different kind of sustenance. Being in man's dimension he couldn't see Pyro approaching, although he felt the heat. "Pyro," he asked, looking around, "what are you doing here?"

Pyro appeared after folding into man's dimension and joining him. "I think the question is, 'What are **you** doing here?'"

"Come on," Perseus urged, "tasting man's food isn't forbidden."

Together the angels tasted the grapes and enjoyed the adventure.

It was Perseus who heard screaming. They didn't have time to return to their eleventh dimension before they saw a woman running from a rebel angel they recognized as Kasdaye. He either did not see them or thought they were men who didn't threaten him. What they saw next horrified them. He was in the process of raping her.

"We can't get involved," Perseus whispered.

"Should we just stand by and do nothing?" Pyro asked.

"Isn't this exactly what Zuben warned us about?" Perseus answered, sweat beads forming on his brow. He saw the woman was beautiful. He understood the attraction.

When Kasdaye was finished, he left her weeping, her face bruised and bloodied from being struck.

"We can comfort her, can't we?" Perseus asked.

Pyro saw no harm in that.

The two approached her and tended to her wounds. Then they wanted to take her to a safe place.

"There is no safe place," the woman sobbed. "My father and brothers are dead. I have no one to protect me."

Perseus' heart wept for her. He could not help returning several times to check on her while he and Pyro carried out their assignments. Sometimes he would reveal himself and other times he would not. He noticed special things about her: her heavy hair flowed down to the hollow in her back, her tiny waist and small wrists. He especially noticed her green eyes against her olive skin and how happy he felt when she laughed. He found himself unhappy when he was not around her. Then he wondered how it all happened, this strange entanglement. He was miserable.

When he and Pyro returned to Ma'on, he knew he needed help. His entire angelic being doubted the wisdom of God, but he had no intentions of becoming a rebel. He didn't know what to do. Finally, he decided to seek help from Auroran.

Confusion
Chapter Fifty-One

Auroran glanced up from his seat in the Honorarium to see Perseus standing before him with the strap of his sword sheath across his loose shirt attached to the belt around his waist. Unlike other warriors, Perseus carried his sword and sheath strapped across his back instead of at his side. He noticed Perseus' face was etched with grief. Auroran set his pen aside and greeted his companion. "Perseus."

"I need to speak with you," Perseus whispered, "I'm in confusion. My heart has been captured by a daughter of a man. Now I burn with questions."

"You know such a union is against the laws of the Heavens," Auroran replied.

"It seems unreasonable to have such a law," Perseus argued. "If you saw her you would agree she is beautiful and much to be desired."

"You know as well as I that it is written in the stones of fire that angels are not to comingle with daughters of men. It is – even as you yourself say – *confusion*."

Silence hung in the air between them.

Auroran felt a refreshing breeze caress his cheek, coming in through the open colonnade full of tall, slender pillars at the back of the building. It helped disperse the silence.

Perseus held his head between his hands.

Auroran felt for him and spoke softly. "Let's assume the Almighty were to suspend this 'unreasonable' law, what then, in your opinion, *should be* taboo? Where should the Almighty draw the line? Should the law allow unions between the living and the dead? Between man and animals? Where would you have the Most High draw the line?"

Perseus diverted the conversation away from a question to an accusation against God. "Why does God allow such suffering among the very creation He claims to love?"

"That question – why God made it so – is not one that I can answer. I believe the real question is: 'Are we going to trust God?' Does He have a reason we do not understand? What if He is protecting rather than punishing?" Auroran paused. He could not divulge that he had his own questions in regard to the plans of God. As he struggled to help Perseus with words of comfort, the arched entrance leading to the Pane Room caught his eye. There, the interactive holographic image of OKUL was available to answer questions requiring deep insight.

Auroran glanced back at Perseus, still in distress. "I've earned two sessions with OKUL." Auroran reached into his pocket to retrieve two metallic "tickets." He slid his sessions across the table. "You need these more than I," he said, nodding toward the Pane Room.

Perseus didn't move. He stared at the sessions lying on the table. "These are valuable, Auroran. I know the angelic service required to earn such as these."

"Now they are yours." Auroran rose. "Hopefully, they will give you the comfort you need."

Perseus rose slowly, still staring at the tickets.

Auroran smiled to see that his newfound friend's grief was now replaced with hope.

Perseus gave Auroran his arm before he left; they joined forearm to forearm, an angelic gesture of affinity.

Would Perseus consider rebelling? Auroran did not know. The daughters of men were only one of many lures Satán used in order to hook angels into rebellion. Auroran sighed deeply as he looked upwards towards Araboth, the seventh Heaven, the dwelling place of the Almighty. Auroran remembered a time when the Heavens were a paradise without rebellion, without grief.

Auroran returned to his task of putting a crew together to chart the universe. Scout angels gathered information, filling in gaps of unknown areas. Auroran sighed, thinking: *Being a scout would have been something Borealis would have thoroughly taken to.*

A Lone Rebel
Chapter Fifty-Two

Auroran took a mental inventory of the angels: Chronos and Kairos were in the Honorarium with D'shubba, Wisdom and Choices were on earth assigning values, Zuben and Menkib were guarding the entrance to the

Garden of Eden, Perseus was in the Pane room with OKUL getting help with his feelings for a woman on earth, Acamar had rebelled, and Pyro was in the temple. So, where was Borealis?

He shook his thoughts aside and surveyed the Honorarium.

D'shubba stood over Chronos' shoulder helping document the events of men. Auroran had been given a new assignment – to study mankind. He noted that Lamech, the newest man child on earth, was born 874 man-years from creation. The earth had aged, but angels had not. Unseen by men, angels zipped through the unknown dimensions of the universe faster than the speed of light.

Men continued to multiply at an astonishing rate. With the multiplication of men also came the multiplication of evil. Auroran spent more and more time studying these men through the writings of the scribes.

Auroran entered the rotunda to join D'shubba reading from Chronos' scroll.

"Greetings, Auroran," D'shubba said, looking up. Taking note of Auroran's slumped appearance D'shubba commented, "Something amiss?"

"Something ... or nothing, I don't know." Auroran couldn't identify the source of his distraction. Perhaps it was the continual turmoil each time Satán appeared in Heaven. *Satán's arrogance was incredible. He not only recruited angels openly but had the audacity to appear before God accusing man! Yet God had taken no action. In spite of all this, God remained silent.*

"I see you are deeply troubled," D'shubba commented.

"Are we not all troubled, D'shubba?" Auroran murmured. "It's been ages since Satán rebelled, yet no communication comes from above. Are you not troubled, D'shubba?" Auroran threw himself into a nearby chair.

"There is a trouble to be endured, and there is a trouble that destroys. Which trouble troubles you?" D'shubba asked, tucking his hands into the openings of his sleeves.

Auroran fumed. *Doubting God now beat at him like whipping winds pummeling the sails of a storm-driven ship.* Auroran moaned inwardly. *Is the Arm of God so short it can take no action? Why does God sit in His temple while violence rages upon the earth? Why is there no action while darkness eats away at the edges of Heaven? How many angels must rebel and how many men perish; how many man-years must pass before something is done?* Question after question struck with the savagery of a hurricane taking vengeance on a flailing ship. *Does Lucifer . . . ha Satán . . . have more authority than Auroran might have realized?* That fleeting thought shook him to his core. Auroran chose not to reply to D'shubba's question. Instead, he focused on his task, which was to relay the names of the angels known to have followed Satán.

Chronos wrote vigorously to keep up with every word.

Auroran opened with, "These are the known rebels and their respective roles:

One: Kasdaye, the angel of demonic practices, formerly the angel of signs and wonders.
Two: Lyrid Mot, the angel of sickness, formerly Lucifer's legal aide.
Three: Etán, the angel of war, formerly the angel of hailstones.
Four: Marcus, the angel of carnal pleasures and addictions, formerly the angel of positive influence.
Five: Acamar, the angel of confusion, formerly an invisible angel, and finally,
Satán, the father of lies, makes six."

Auroran continued. "These are the rebel angels in Satán's hierarchy. Other lower angels are being enlisted by this hierarchy. Their names will be relayed shortly." Auroran paused. Grief filled his heart as he looked at his friends, the angels sitting at the table. "Let this teach us to look after our brother angels. We need to reach out and protect each other. The attraction of Satán is strong."

"Is this the question of the bottomless pit we discussed earlier?" D'shubba asked calmly.

"Yes," Auroran heaved. "Neediness is a black hole. It pulls light into it and imprisons it forever. Its pull is ferocious."

"Yes, yes, of course," the distracted D'shubba answered. D'shubba rose and returned to examine Chronos' scroll sprawled out on a table before them. Each scroll had been titled with one identifiable man-year. These scrolls were kept in numerical order. Chronos worked on scroll number 874.

When D'shubba finished, Chronos unrolled a separate scroll for Auroran. The scrolls were written vertically with a chronology of man-days in the left column and each day's events on the right.

"Good ... good," Auroran commented. "It is amazing how men have multiplied in spite of their miserable conditions. It's like a pot of stew."

Auroran scanned the scroll; he saw the birth and death of every man, woman, and child ... and the events and works of the multitudes. "Very clever," Auroran commented. "But what about studying the events in just one person's life? Would we have to search the scrolls to pick out events pertaining to just one person?"

"No, indeed," D'shubba said. He led Auroran through an archway toward another scribe. "What you are describing is the work of Kairos and his staff. There is one scribe assigned to each man. They not only write the chronology of events for each person but add the divine moments of God working in each one's life. Each person has one angel assigned to him or her."

Auroran knew the work of the scribes was daunting. As men multiplied, so did the work of the angels. Auroran now oversaw legions of scribes. He stayed with Chronos to complete the list of every angel known to have rebelled and to whom each reported.

Transplant
Chapter Fifty-Three

Perseus and Pyro had returned to earth to retrieve the Tree of Life from the Garden of Eden without Zuben or Menkib knowing their activities. This would be the last trip for their assignment on earth. Perseus sought out Zillah, the daughter of a man with whom he was smitten. Upon finding her he was surprised to find she had aged, although she was still beautiful. Neither he nor Pyro revealed themselves, but they watched with interest. Perseus' heart had not stopped aching for her. She was crouching behind a fallen tree wedged on a large rock. At first they thought she was gathering food until they saw Kasdaye approaching.

It became obvious Zillah was hiding from Kasdaye.

Pyro quickly folded himself into man's dimensions and threw a rock where the sound drew Kasdaye away from her.

Kasdaye turned to follow the sound of the stone's rustling in the brush.

Pyro continued throwing rocks in the bushes, here and there. Then Perseus followed Pyro's lead. Together they led Kasdaye far away from Zillah.

When Kasdaye spotted them, he was shocked to discover the two angels from Heaven there. "If the hierarchy were here—"

"If the hierarchy were here," Pyro interrupted, "you wouldn't be following your evil intent."

"You are not allowed to interfere," Kasdaye reminded them. "Aren't you are out of your element?"

Perseus grinned. "We are wandering and exploring."

Kasdaye shot back, "Be grateful I'm alone."

"And you are in danger," Pyro countered, "in danger of hell fire."

Kasdaye, miffed, turned and left.

Both Perseus and Pyro knew it would be Zillah who would pay the price for Kasdaye's humiliation. They knew as soon as they left, Kasdaye would return and go after her. Furthermore, if they stayed, he would return with more rebel angels and their own existence would be in danger.

"What do we do?" Perseus asked Pyro.

"Let's pretend we've left," Pyro offered.

Together the angels folded themselves back into their eleventh dimension and left, flying away in a pattern that would appear as if they had left earth for the Heavens. Away from earth, Perseus and Pyro began questioning why God allowed this. *Why didn't He protect His creation?* As they circled back to earth, they saw Kasdaye pulling Zillah from her hiding place.

Perseus had never seen Pyro so angry, but warned: "Don't interfere, Pyro."

Pyro stayed back, but his anger multiplied in his face. Seeing Kasdaye torture Zillah, Pyro wondered if he knew they were watching.

Without warning Pyro took out after Kasdaye. The two fought in hand-to-hand combat scorching the earth. Then the battle lifted up into the air and out into the atmosphere. Perseus watched the two balls of fire, unable to keep up with the fight. He took off to help, but the fight was now on man's moon as angel fought angel leaving scars over the forested moon, now ablaze. Once again the angels rose, this time facing each other, sword against sword. The battle worked its way toward the sun. Its heat sapped Kasdaye of his strength but filled Pyro with new, vibrant energy.

Finally Kasdaye left. Pyro, panting, returned to Perseus.

"What have you done?" Perseus yelled at his friend. "You will be brought before the Council!"

Pyro looked at Perseus in defiance, breathing heavily. "I'm not returning."

"What?" Perseus couldn't believe him. "You must return. Are you going to join that monster?"

"I'll hide out," Pyro answered.

"And what? Become a pirate angel?" Perseus couldn't believe his friend.

"If God isn't going to help, then I will," Pyro answered. "I no longer trust God and I can't hide it."

"And I can't leave you here," Perseus insisted.

"Then you will have to catch me." At that Pyro zoomed away. Perseus followed until he had no idea where his friend had gone. There was no other option but to return to the Heavens with the Tree of Life, but without Pyro.

Provision
Chapter Fifty-Four

After returning, Perseus spent much time in the temple trying to forget what had transpired on earth with Pyro.

Auroran, after hearing the story from Perseus, was eager to learn and tell Perseus that Zillah had married one called Lamech.

When Perseus heard the news, he was relieved. "Now Kasdaye will leave her be. God provided her with a protector." Perseus took a deep breath before telling Auroran Pyro had rebelled.

"Have you heard from Pyro since then?" Auroran asked.

"I've only heard about him," Perseus answered. "His attacks against the rebels are becoming renown in the heavens. When Pyro encounters a rebel unaccompanied by other rebels, he slays them with their own seeds of lies. The lies are darts that force a sickening rest. Angels melt and have difficulty reviving. Angels who do not wish to join Satán but no longer trust God are joining him. Strange, isn't it – rebel fighting rebel."

Auroran shook his head. *They were all rebels who did not rely on the Lord.*

Desolation
Chapter Fifty-Five

Borealis woke from his drug-induced state to find himself as nothing more than a crumpled bundle lying on a slimy green ledge, encapsulated in darkness. Shivering from a cold draft, he realized he was without his robe. *The scuffle must have torn it off.* The green, slimy walls at his back left him cold – very, very cold. The pit emitted a fetid odor of rank mold. The light within his angelic body was fading. He fumbled, reaching out with his hands to feel the perimeter of the ledge.

Winds howled from far below raised worrisome sounds of moaning and groaning. *Were there other creatures in this pit?* It was all he could do to stay on the slippery ledge. He did not have the capacity to fly or move at the speed of light. He had no choice but to sit in darkness and wait – with no concept of earthly days or earthly nights or the passing of events in Heaven. Timelessness was his worst enemy.

Concentrate, he told himself, *just concentrate.*

As tired as he was, Borealis knew he had to stay alert. Fear ripped at him causing him to jerk spasmodically. He needed rest. His angelic body cried out for it. He fought to keep himself together. The more exhausted he became, the more he had to force himself not to slip into his rest. If he were to melt into liquid light, he would be lost to the pit. He began to see strange things that made no sense. When he jerked to full consciousness, panic dripped from his sweating, clammy, cold body.

Something unnatural seemed to whisper in his ear, or was it is own voice? *Since God is sovereign, and God allowed this, then God must be sadistic.*

No, no, Borealis told himself. *All this is not real. This darkness has no reality of its own.*

His throat swelled. Surely, fear had crawled inside his throat. Panic caused him to gasp for air. Again, sinister thoughts whispered in and around his ear. *"If this is not real, then why are you here? Where is this 'Light' that you cling to? Let go ... do not resist."*

Borealis' eyes rolled upward into his head. "Light is truth," he whispered, "therefore, darkness is a lie."

Fear had now enlarged itself in his belly, ripping his inner being apart with the savagery of a rapacious beast. He realized his fear must have come from Satán's drink, tainted with Satán's lies. He desperately clung to the dark, dank ledge he crouched upon.

His sanity was slipping away. With his small reserve of energy, he found himself yelling at the echoing chamber, "Retreat, you slithering gray shadow of a serpent, you coward! You are powerless against Light!" After a pause, he whispered to himself. "Just as darkness cannot prevail over Light, lies cannot prevail over Truth. If you must fear, fear God – and God alone."

He startled. A rumbling came from below that shook the walls. Then, an enormous "whoosh" passed by, unlike the forces of any wind he had ever known, so stiff it almost knocked him off his ledge. He shook his head, wondering, *What was that?*

Relieved
Chapter Fifty-Six

On the face of the earth at the entrance to the Garden of Eden, a captain in the Lord's service arrived to give Zuben and Menkib their new assignments. He was accompanied by a handful of other warrior angels. Menkib was the first to be told.

"Zuben! We are relieved of our duties to return to the City of God, to *Ma'on*!" Menkib put his sword away. The swooshing of his sword was silenced. An eerie silence ensued when both swords stopped swooshing. There was silence for the first time in ages, a welcome relief to both Zuben and Menkib.

Menkib eagerly received his new assignment from the captain.

"Yes, it's true," the captain assured them. "You both have been reassigned," he smiled as he produced the first of two medallions. "Well done, Menkib." The captain put his finger on his forehead then snapped it outwards towards Menkib in a salute of trust and honor. "You have earned this medallion that honors your service." He showed it to Menkib. "I have been instructed to place it on you at the next Assembly in the presence of witnesses, so that you can say 'I have been honored by the Almighty.'"

Menkib did not try to hide his jubilation. He remembered the many times he believed he would not be able to finish this assignment.

Zuben walked over to his friend and examined the medallion. "Well done, Menkib!" Zuben rejoiced with his friend. "And a promotion, too!"

"What about Zuben's medallion?" Menkib asked, puzzled.

"I'm sure the captain has a medallion for me as well," Zuben smiled.

The captain nodded in affirmation as he produced a similar medallion and presented it to Zuben.

Zuben received his next assignment from the captain, read it, then re-read it. "I would like to take time to enjoy this last moment." Zuben stretched and walked about. "You two go ahead and return to the city of God without me," he told them. "I want to stay and do some exploring."

"But it's not safe for you to be alone here," Menkib protested.

"I won't be long," Zuben insisted. "This moment fills me with a headiness I can't resist!"

"I understand," Menkib replied. "Let me stay with you."

"No," Zuben insisted. "I really would like some time here alone."

Menkib finally gave in. "Have it your way. But I don't like it. You know as well as I that it's dangerous for you to be here alone."

Zuben patted his friend on his back. "Thank you for your concern. But I am not a weak angel. I doubt I will be confronted by Satán's rebel angels."

Reluctantly, Menkib gave Zuben his arm to bid him farewell. Menkib stretched his unused wings, spreading them and testing them before flying off with the captain and the hosts of warriors.

Zuben waited and watched until they disappeared from sight.

Frogs
Chapter Fifty-Seven

Borealis knew he was in trouble; he could no longer hang on. How long had he been there – minutes, hours, ages? How many events in heaven and earth had passed? Had any? He knew the bottomless pit was dead center in Hades, right in the middle of Satán's headquarters. *Dead South of True North*, he joked half-heartedly, *pun intended*. He trembled. He couldn't make it. He was losing himself. He felt ready to liquefy. It took all his energy to hold himself together. He began to imagine how his end might come as he saw himself dripping over the edge of the ledge, caught by the draft to be blown about, his form lost forever to the winds of avarice, greed, and corruption. If he melted, he wouldn't have enough light to pull his form back together again.

Was he hallucinating, or did he see the eyes of a frog-like creature? Not one, but three! What other creatures might be in here? "Who are you?" he whispered.

"We are three unclean spirits," the largest frog croaked, "We produce venom for the serpent. Touch us and melt, eat us and die."

The second frog corrected the first frog, "Except for the serpent. The serpent is immune from our poison."

Then the third frog added, "But not entirely immune."

Borealis sat isolated in the pit, shaking his head. His eyes rolled backwards. He strained to keep his form together, expending every ounce of the last of his energy. *What was to become of him?* He found himself moaning like the sounds that rose from below. *This must be what it is like to be human – lost, alone, hopeless, abandoned.* This bottomless pit was a place of isolation, abandonment, deprivation. His heart began to ache. He found he could bear it no longer. He would have to let go. He felt a drop of something splatter on his knee. *What was that?* He shivered at the core of his being. Was it water, or was it another angel who had been trapped on a ledge from above who could no longer hold on and who melted into blobs of nothingness?

Exhausted, he was now ready to let loose. Just as he was ready to let go he felt an Arm grab him and pull him through a door, a door that existed only from the outside and not from the inside. He fainted as he heard another "whoosh" roar around the hollowness of the pit.

When he opened his eyes on the outside of the pit an unknown angel of Light stood over him, supporting him, strengthening him.

"Bless you!" Borealis whispered. "I was not able to hold on any longer."

Satán's Shame
Chapter Fifty-Eight

Adam was an old man. Although Eve had died, he continued to fight with the ground in order to feed himself and others.

Not a mist, but a strange steam rose from the earth draining Adam of his strength.

Adam struggled as he tried to pull a bush's roots from the hard soil using a rope made from the twisted wool of Abel's sheep. Abel's wool was stronger than any vine. He kept trying to clear the land. He did not know the steam being emitted in the eleventh dimension was the result of heat from an army of rebels beneath the earth. All Adam knew after Abel's death was the hard, repetitive work gave him only the barest emotional relief. He wished with all his heart he had been the one to die instead of Abel. Eve had changed. Her passion had turned to dust. It wasn't her fault. He blamed himself. Sometimes the pain of failure was more than he could bear; it rose in his chest to overtake him. He beat his fist against a tree without any inclination Satán was standing directly behind him, invisible, whispering failure in his ear.

Black, ugly seeds of lies swarmed from Satán's mouth into Adam's ear. "It's your fault your son is dead. If you had not eaten the fruit from the Tree of Good and Evil - If you had resisted, everything would be as it was before. Because of your weakness, one son is dead and the other is marked as a criminal. All your descendants are doomed. Eve has refused you, not willing to give her strength to you. You are the worst of failures."

Adam lost his temper. He raised his man-made hoe high above his head and beat the ground until it broke, then throwing himself on the ground. He shouted at God at the top of his voice: "Can You see me?" He beat on his chest with his open hand. "Can You hear me? I am riddled with pain! Do You care? I lie here in anguish of soul ... my heart is torn open. My dignity bleeds into the earth where I cannot gather it. Why won't You answer me? Won't You give me one moment of relief? Oh my God, do not forsake me!"

Satán laughed. He watched Adam radiate with pain as he continued to twist him without compassion. He tore at Adam's emotions, feasting on his pain.

"Why do you do that, Satán?" Zuben spoke out. "Why do you torment this old man? Surely he cannot be a threat to you."

Startled to see Zuben, Satán's eyes smoldered. "So you *are* here my friend! Etán told me so, but I didn't believe him. Are you here to report on me?"

"You couldn't be more wrong. I am not here to report on you, Satán, but if such an assignment had been offered, I would dutifully accept." Zuben returned Satán's comments with contempt. "As for friendship, you and I both know friends have each other's best interest at heart. I don't believe a friend you ever were."

"So," Satán simmered, "then we each know where the other stands."

Tear Drop
Chapter Fifty-Nine

Zuben turned toward his foe. "You have earned your name *the Accuser*. Today I have witnessed it. You are no longer a bearer of light. It saddens me to see your darkness. The Lord has given you a new name: Desolation. You are the fallen angel of desolation and destruction."

Satán scoffed at his foe. "You can do nothing without God's permission. I, on the other hand, have the freedom to follow my will. I can leave if I choose or stay if I so desire. At this moment I have the ability either to slay you or to elevate you." Satán continued to pontificate, although his voice softened. "What do you think, Zuben? Follow me and experience this freedom yourself! Can't you see that it is you who are operating in darkness? How can you make a decision without trying this for yourself? See?"

"Freedom under you *is* bondage," Zuben rebutted. Bondage under God is freedom. If I transgress God's divine laws then I become a slave of sin. Those who follow you have been trapped by your lies. I decline your offer."

"Well, then, I leave you in good stead, Zuben. I believe you will come to your senses. Consider my offer; it is a good one and one that many of your friends are accepting."

Zuben refused to dispute with him. "The Lord rebuke you."

"Very well, but the offer stays open. I'll be here when you are ready to follow me." Satán curled his lip and disappeared. When he was out of sight, he quickly retrieved Adam's hue he had hid from Zuben and gorged on it voraciously. He did not want Zuben to see his weakness. It was humiliating to feed like pigs on the hue of men.

Zuben continued his walk east into the dangerous territory of Nod where many fallen angels had congregated. He successfully remained undetected until he found what he was looking for. Buried in tall grass was a stone marking the grave of Beth. She was so beautiful and Marcus had ruined her. Zuben grieved for her spirit. He admired her spunk. Because of Marcus she fell into a terrible and brutal life. Zuben spoke of it to no one, not even Menkib, but watching Beth being brutalized had become the hardest part of his assignment. He could not interfere. He felt a tear run down his face and watched as it dropped on her gravestone.

The tear on the gravestone did not dissipate. It hardened into a permanent drop of glassy dew catching the rays of the sun. On this bright day, it sparkled like a diamond.

Finding Eve's Descendent
Chapter Sixty

As time passed and men multiplied on the earth, Auroran was faithful to document the names of men, the sons of men and the sons of the sons of men. Auroran wrote:

"Adam's son was Seth and Seth's son was Enosh. Enosh grew and had a son and named him Cainan, Cainan had a son and named him Mahalalel, Mahalalel had Jared, Jared had Enoch who pleased God, Enoch had Methuselah, and Methuselah had Lamech (who lived at the same time as the Lamech who married Zillah). Lamech, the son of Methuselah had Noah and Noah married the daughter of Lamech and Zillah, whose name is Naamah."

Auroran noticed a sentence in the meanings of their names:
Adam means "Man," Seth means "Appointed Substitute," Enosh means "Mortal," Cainan means "Sorrow," Mahalalel means "The blessed God," Jared means "Shall come down," Enoch means "Teaching," Methuselah means "His death shall bring," Lamech means "Despairing," and Noah means "Comfort and Rest."

Auroran puzzled over the string of these names. Put together they said "(A) man (is to be an) appointed substitute (for) mortal sorrow. The blessed God shall come down teaching. His death shall bring (the) despairing comfort and rest."

The sentence, as it stood seemed to have no meaning to Auroran. As he puzzled over it he was unexpectedly interrupted.

"I see you're still wielding your weapon of choice," Zuben joked as he approached, pointing toward Auroran's quill.

Auroran jumped up and embraced Zuben.

Together the angels sat down at the table where Zuben took Auroran's quill and examined it.

"Ah, my quill, of course." Auroran watched Zuben examine the details of his pen: The long extended feathers, the ornate nib, the handle of pure gold, and all the elaborate motifs. Such a pen reflected Auroran's lofty position in the kingdom of God. "But nothing compared to your sword, Zuben."

Zuben pulled his sword from its sheath and lay it beside Auroran's pen. "This sword releases its power when wielded by love. You and I wield the weapons of God's Truth." Zuben gave his sword a fancy swoosh before returning it to his sheath. "With your pen and my sword we are both warriors, each in our own way."

"Indeed." Auroran smiled, elated to have Zuben back. "Your assignment is finished?"

"Yes," Zuben grinned. "But I still have to submit my report."

Both angels rose, gave each other their arm, then Zuben left.

After the departure of Zuben, an angelic messenger startled everyone when he swept through the Honorarium to land in front of Auroran. Everyone stopped their work to hear the news. It must be important if it could not wait for an assembly.

Enoch
Chapter Sixty-One

"The man Enoch is here, right here – on the mountain of God," the messenger gushed. "He did not die. God brought him here." The breathless messenger rose to leave. "I must go, there are others to tell."

"But wait!" Auroran cried out. "Surely, there is more. Where is he? Is he in the temple? Is there a reason for this? What does it mean?"

"There is no other information, only that which you now know. If you wish, go to the arena. Many angels are gathering there. They may have more."

D'shubba and Auroran looked at each other in bewilderment trying to make sense of this news.

Auroran knew Enoch was one of the descendants of Seth he had just documented: "Jared had Enoch who pleased God."

Kairos proclaimed, "This is a divine moment!" He quickly penned the information.

Chronos also took to scribbling feverishly: "In the 987th year from creation, Enoch, in his 365th man-year, being a man of God, has been taken to the third heaven. Born from the line of Seth, the son of Adam...." Chronos noticed the Honorarium was quiet. He glanced up to see that D'shubba, Auroran, and Kairos were gone. The Honorarium was empty. Chronos dropped his quill and ran after them.

Seven Golden Arches
Chapter Sixty-Two

The angels were given no other information concerning Enoch nor did any angel see him in the Heavens.

Auroran was invited to serve as a temple angel and viewed it as a blessing. Eager to serve, he floated through the two gates leading into the temple of glory.

On this occasion, he especially needed the peace. Upon entering, he felt grace all around him. He was uplifted as he heard the song of the angels. His heart was light. He worshipped in joy, peace, and understanding. In the chanting of the canticles he understood God's love for mankind.

A temple angel approached with a censer swinging in his hand. In its wake, a sweet perfume filled the temple. Auroran took it in, savoring the heady aroma.

"I am Tyl, your instructor," the temple angel introduced himself.

"What is this aromatic perfume?" Auroran asked.

"It is the prayers of men," Tyl answered. "Follow me." He walked to a short pillar in the middle of the room, set the censer down, then opened the censer. He poured a potion from a vial before sprinkling something on the prayers. A smoky incense rose higher and higher filling the temple.

"What did you add to the prayers?" Auroran asked curiously.

"Dry blood," Tyl answered.

"Blood?" Auroran puzzled.

"It comes to us from the throne room," Tyl continued.

Auroran looked around. His reflection showed on the gleaming granite floor.

"The floor is the footstool of our Lord," Tyl informed him. "It is the face of the earth. Your assignment is to stand upon the face of the earth and offer heavenward the prayers of men. These prayers ascend into the throne room of the Almighty."

Auroran was glad he could not hear these prayers, for he knew they were heavy with grief. Only a few had the heady aroma of praise.

By the time he left his duties, he felt his joy could not be diminished. He looked forward to seeing Menkib now that Menkib had returned from his assignment on earth. He thought about flying, but he wanted to conserve his energy. Since he chose to walk, he hastened his step.

Auroran followed the Path of Life to the great seven arches of heaven. As he approached the arches, he noticed a great deal of activity taking place around the Fifth Great Arch. Angels floated in and out of the convergence of energy that appeared as a great white pearl. As Auroran neared, an angel of authority banned him from entering. *Banned?* Auroran puzzled. *What does this mean?*

Auroran bypassed the arches to enter the Forest of Wisdom. Beyond the forest, in the far distance, he saw smoke rising from the Eternal Stones of Fire where Lucifer had spent his time learning the laws.

He crossed from the mainland to Makon by walking over a bridge connecting the two islands of heaven. Makon was a land of rocks on its outer perimeter, but its interior was flush with a forgotten forested region. Auroran arrived at the storehouses of God where Menkib had been reassigned. There, great blessings were being stored for those whom God chose to favor. Conversely, there were also hailstones, water, and fire piled in reserve for a day of judgment. Auroran shuddered at the thought of God's wrath, but he would not allow these thoughts to temper his anticipation of meeting Menkib who had come out to greet him.

"Come, Auroran!" Menkib beamed upon catching sight of his friend. "Walk with me!"

"Joy and peace, Menkib!" Auroran reciprocated as he joined his friend, the two walking side by side. "Tell me about this storehouse in which you now serve."

"There isn't much to tell. God has hemmed in the waters of the deep, fire is contained in the furnace of wrath, and stockpiles of hailstones weighing 75 pounds each are being kept in reserve." Menkib turned to Auroran to talk to him in earnest. "You would not believe the foul odor of man's sin on earth. The stench is abhorrent. Surely, God must see the wickedness of man on earth. The descendants of those unions between rebel angels and the daughters of men continue to multiply, choking out the bloodline of man. Violence flows; blood fills every crack and crevice in the earth. Can God make everything right again?"

Auroran shook his head sadly. "I watch from the arena. The skies teem with black clouds of fallen angels. They swarm like flies, destroy like locusts, and sting like wasps. I'm happy the Lord has brought you back. Who knows what might have become of you?"

"I am waiting to hear from Zuben," Menkib replied.

"He has returned and you will see him soon. As for me, I am waiting to hear from Borealis." Auroran moaned. "No one has seen or heard from him."

Signs of Wrath
Chapter Sixty-Three

Auroran' concern for his brother deepened after seeing Menkib. He chose to believe Borealis was continuing his quest to explore the universe. He desired to talk to his brother, to share news, to simply visit. But his brother consistently seemed to be out of communication.

Entering the Honorarium and taking his seat, Auroran prepared his quill to write his scheduled report:

> "By the will of God and in His Service, I, Auroran, the angel in whom God has entrusted the Eternal Ring of Keys, do once again set my hand to journal the following accounts relating to the wars among men and angels:
>
> On the mountain of God, Satán uses persuasive words dipped in the poisons of flattery and lies to seduce the ranks of angels. By present count, millions have fallen. Their names are listed in *The Wars of the LORD*.
>
> Earth does not escape his agenda of putrescent carnage: War and destruction work as flint and tender, spreading fires of violence across the landscape of the earth. Disease scatters forth her seeds of misery reaping the deaths of the hapless masses. The pillars of Justice and Mercy lie in ruins. The oaks of natural affection are choked out by vines of vile, detestable pleasures that twist the soul and distort the hearts of men.

From unthinkable to unimaginable, it is reported fallen angels have used their powers to take the daughters of men to themselves for their pleasure, producing unnatural offspring.

Satán spends his time scouring the face of the earth, searching for the prophesied descendent of Eve who will crush his head. To this task the fallen ones have been commissioned to search without ceasing.

Signs of God's impending wrath are growing. They express themselves in claps of thunder that shake the Heavens. His storehouses are filled with hailstones, water, and fire. He will surely bring victory out of thwarted justice.

The Lord is exalted, sitting high and lifted up. The train of His authority fills the temple. The Lord is slow to anger, gracious and merciful – but He will *not at all* acquit the wicked.

I, Auroran, swear by Him who lives forever and forever that this report is just and true. Power and Glory and Honor to Him who was, and is, and is to come, the Almighty.

His Dutiful Servant,

Auroran."

Seventy Times Seven
Chapter Sixty-Four

Lamech, who was the fifth from Cain, staggered in from the fields covered in blood. His wives, Adah and Zillah, upon seeing him, ran to him and helped him back to their tents.

"What is it my husband? What has happened?" Adah asked above his weeping and lamenting while Zillah lowered him onto a covering.

"Forgive me! Forgive me!" he cried aloud reaching for the heavens.

"Forgive you, for what?" Adah persistently asked, anxious to know what had happened, but Lamech was hysterical.

Zillah and her daughter Naamah wetted rags, already busy wiping blood from Lamech.

"Naamah," Zillah instructed, "Go fetch your brothers - Jabal, Jubal, and Tubal-Cain."

Naamah went out immediately, for her father's cries were severe.

"I am surely the offspring of Cain!" Lamech wailed, "Even as said."

Both Adah and Zillah tried to piece together his story within his babbling all the while cleaning blood from his body. They found no wound.

"Adah and Zillah, stop now! Hear me; you wives of Lamech, listen to me!" Lamech sobbed violently, "I killed a man for wounding me, he was only a young man but he hurt me."

Adah and Zillah listened quietly, now that their husband was making a semblance of sense.

"If Cain is avenged sevenfold, then I seventy-sevenfold. Can God forgive Lamech seventy times seven?"

Naamah, upon finding her brother Tubal-Cain, rushed back with him to comfort their father.

An Offer
Chapter Sixty-Five

Auroran hurried to make it to the Assembly Hall for the scheduled Assembly of Advancements. Menkib and Zuben were to receive their medals and honors. In spite of the celebration, he found it difficult to enjoy the ceremonies because his mind was on his brother. Auroran received neither medallion nor promotion at this assembly. It was true he had done his duties as an angel, but he had not extended himself as honor would warrant.

After the ceremony, outside the Assembly Hall, he saw Zuben. "Congratulations, Zuben!" he said with a smile. "You are now the Commander of the LORD's army!"

"The Lord God has decreed that it is so. We are to have an army after all." He lowered his voice. "Tell me, have you heard from your brother?"

"No. He is adventurous, as you know." Auroran found himself prattling to cover his concerns for his capricious, absent brother. "You know Borealis. He spends his time hurling through the universe." The two angels shared a laugh.

"I could use him in my service," Zuben said. "Please let him know he has an offer when you see him."

Borealis? An offer to serve in the Lord's army? Auroran was delighted, "Yes, I will tell him straightway when I see him."

Even as they spoke, other angels gathered around Zuben waiting to offer their blessings, goodwill, and honor.

Auroran admired Zuben. His medallions were a testament to his strength, loyalty, and devotion. He had earned them. *Zuben is a strong angel.*

After leaving the Assembly Hall, Auroran decided to go to the arena. He wanted to see if he could find the face of his brother, but it was nowhere to be seen. After an inordinate amount of time watching Corona, Auroran was startled when a second angel entered. Auroran immediately recognized his friend. "Menkib! Good company enters."

"Fresh from promotions," Menkib replied, half smiling. "No promotion for you, Auroran?"

"Most of the time I find I am distracted."

"As am I," Menkib said. "The storehouse speaks of the troubles that lie ahead."

"What brings you here to the arena?" Auroran asked his friend.

"I wanted to talk to you," Menkib answered. "Are you aware Satán visited me for recruitment?"

Auroran raised his eyebrows. "No, I wasn't."

"Yes," Menkib continued. "He intercepted me as I was about to enter Ma'on."

"At least you were able to resist," Auroran said, hesitating. His statement was more of a question.

"Yes, of course, but I don't understand why the Almighty allows him the freedom to roam heaven. It also causes me to wonder how many others he has approached. I no longer know who I can and *cannot* trust." Menkib's voice trailed off.

"I assume the best in every angel unless I am shown otherwise," Auroran said. "Otherwise, I would be caught in every web of suspicion that Satán throws out."

"I see your point, Auroran. That is wisdom and I thank you." Menkib appreciated his friend's understanding.

"Satán does seem to be working his way up heaven's hierarchy," Auroran commented, fearful for all angels in Satán's path of destruction.

Promoting Evil
Chapter Sixty-Six

Akkamar tired of Satán's non-stop tirades. His vainglorious meanderings, boastful malarkey, and gasconade had ceased making sense. The group's celebrated leader did not follow through with promises, instead, he used recruited angels to search for a mythological descendent of Eve whom God had said would bruise his head. He even convinced Kasdaye to perform demonic practices of voodoo to ward off this supposed prophecy. At each meeting, he devoted an inordinate amount of time on genealogies, hunting down any man who might be suspicious, then plaguing or killing him.

Now, however, Akkamar sighed in relief that at long last they would achieve something at each meeting of the hierarchy. They agreed to share attack strategies.

Kasdaye presented their first strategy. He was their chemist. Every rebel knew about fear and how to use it, but it was Kasdaye who learned its source. From his work in his laboratory he discovered lies were the source of fear. The more lies used, the more mankind feared.

The second presenter, at this meeting, was Marcus, the angel of unnatural pleasures and addictions.

Marcus busily set up an easel for his presentation. His theme was presenting *The Cycle of Addiction in Battered Women and How to Use It*.

Marcus announced he would explain why battered women return to their perpetrators for more beatings.

The group leaned in keen with interest.

"It's a matter of spiritual physics," Marcus explained. "The human soul needs affirmation, nurturing, meaning, and dignity. I would go so far as to say that man's umbilical cord to his Creator is dignity. My plan of attack has been to sever that cord of dignity."

Marcus looked each rebel in the eye around the table. "If I plant a lie in the male perpetrator's mind, like this...." Marcus picked out a black, spiky, metallic seed and held it up between his thumb and forefinger for the group to see. He then picked up a fabricated bubble representing man's soul and placed the seed within the bubble as he continued. "The lie, when it begins to sprout, tells the man something like this: 'Real men are able to control their women. If your woman doesn't do as told, it makes you look the fool.' The perpetrator then begins to believe anything the woman does against his will is done purposely to make him look weak, unmanly, and foolish. So he beats her to affirm his manhood."

Marcus paused while the hierarchy absorbed his words. "Now, this is the best part: The woman, when she is beaten and degraded, believes she is of no value. Without a sense of value, her soul becomes a spiritual vacuum of neediness. In the same way a starved man must have food, her dignity must have affection, affirmation, and acceptance. Therefore, she must 'fix' his bad opinion of her in order to get what she needs. She *is compelled* to convince her batterer that she *does* have worth. She keeps returning to him for affirmation. She will continually ask, 'Am I OK now?' But the answer will always be another beating with fists, whips, or words because he needs to control her. At each and every beating the need is greater, driving her to prove her worth even more. A cycle of addiction has been created in which she can never leave until she feels good about herself – and that never happens. She is inexorably addicted to her perpetrator."

"Brilliant! Brilliant!" Satán pounded his hand on the table, giving his approval.

"But since we do not know the thoughts of a man or a woman," Etán demanded, "how do you know this is so? How do you know what the needs of the human soul are?"

"I plant the lie," Marcus announced, his tone boastful, "the physics take over, and I record the results."

"My presentation will be much easier," Etán said, sneering. "Men kill each other for greed and power."

"Only if I spellbind them first with imaginary offenses," Kasdaye added.

Satán interjected a question to interrupt the members' bickering. "Marcus, can your theory be used in other situations?"

"Yes, it holds true for any people-pleasing situation." Marcus turned to Kasdaye, "You will find it helpful in creating cults. People need someone to tell them they have worth. Plant a lie that says 'you are not valuable' and watch how they eagerly search out a leader who controls them in return for affirmation."

"This is useless stuff for me," Etán complained, "Such a small amount of violence."

"Think of a large cult following their leader." Marcus eagerly responded. "Then imagine a leader who tells them all to commit suicide or face exclusion. Would they?"

Etán rubbed his square chin. "I believe I could give it a try."

"How would I use this technique?" The withered Lyrid Mot propelled his question into the now enthusiastic group.

"Think of a mother who feels ignored and invisible," Marcus responded. "In order to get the affirmation she needs from others – that she is a *good* mother, she becomes willing to make her children sick, pretending to nurture them to get praises from others."

"And me?" Akkamar spoke up.

"The human soul cannot be annihilated, but it can be destroyed inwardly in innumerable ways. Keep affirmation away and you do damage to dignity; we all know a lack of dignity creates chaos and insanity in anyone seeking approval. Go to any reunion and you are bound to come across needy souls looking to their peers to find out if they are 'OK now.'" The answer will always be a resounding "NO!" because anyone seeking approval will always be taken advantage of. No human will lower himself enough to pick the other one up."

Marcus turned and addressed the group. "In summary: All lies tell men they are worthless, which ultimately destroys their dignity."

The group responded to Marcus with hearty applause.

"I thank you!" He beamed.

Satán jumped out of his seat. "We must get our manufacturing plant busy. We must distort more truths into lies. We will get these miserable people to believe that being a 'victim' is somehow 'spiritual.'"

Akkamar pleaded, "So, then, mustn't we stop using recruits to chase genealogies and instead put them to work making lies?"

"No! No!" Satán argued. "I cannot take rebels away from finding the One descendent who is prophesied to be my Destroyer. That task cannot cease! God, however, has stationed the Tinker angel, Jo'el, in Paradise to study men's souls and he has finished his first volume. It would be an easy task to steal his book, *The Physics of Man's Invisible Soul*. That tome would help us understand how to implement and market Marcus' plan of using lies to wreak havoc upon earth. If we go to Heaven together to steal the book and do it quickly, we could get out before we're noticed."

"We could also get arrested and executed if discovered," Marcus murmured.

It Happened
Chapter Sixty-Seven

Auroran left on a trip to visit the edge of the Sea of Nothingness. There, he enjoyed the serenity as he listened to wave after wave crash against the Stones of Fire. Upon these stones the Laws and Ordinances of God were inscribed. The peace was so calming he found himself gazing deep in mindless thought as he sat on the edge of one of the boulders of fire. He didn't mind when his form gave way to a liquid rest bubbling around the heat of the fire.

As he rose from his pool of light to return to his form his arms stretched out to receive this glorious new beginning. Bright and refreshed, he praised God for the peace in the core of his being. He sang songs of worship, his routine of joy. A rest always renewed his strength and gratitude.

Auroran walked along the boulders before pausing and leaning against a balustrade overlooking the sea. He gazed at the waters of nothingness lapping against the shores of Heaven. He wondered if "nothing" was "something," or if "nothing" was simply "nothing"? He decided he would pose that problem to OKUL when he returned to Ma'on.

Out of the corner of his eye he caught a glimpse of an angel racing toward him from his left. The angel was running faster than the speed of light. As he turned to look, he saw it was Menkib, whose face was flushed with horror. Auroran froze – trying to fathom why Menkib would have searched him out at such a distance, all the way from Makon, from God's warehouses. Flying consumed so much energy most angels chose to walk, but it was evident Menkib had flown the entire distance.

"It happened!" Menkib gasped. "It has happened! A messenger angel was dispatched, but I had to come and tell you myself!"

"What?" Auroran coaxed him. "What is it, Menkib?"

"I went to the storehouse," Menkib gasped, "and the waters of the deep were gone ... *empty!* So I ran to the arena, and ... well, there you are!"

"I'm sorry, Menkib, I don't understand."

"Come back to the city of God, to the arena. I'll show you!"

Auroran and Menkib flew to the arena spending all their energy, wasting no time.

Auroran was glad he had rested so he had enough power to fly.

When they finally reached Ma'on, from overhead, Auroran saw angels rushing to the arena. In spite of the crowds, Menkib and Auroran made their way inside.

"Look!" Menkib said. "A comet has pierced the earth's canopy of ice, crashing the icy water onto the earth. It hit the earth and opened the chambers of waters lying beneath the earth's crust."

Auroran was aghast; he could not pull his eyes away from the disaster he was witnessing. The waters from above were gushing down onto the earth. Water chambers from below the earth's crust were breaking open, violently spewing waters from the deep, sweeping men, women, children, and animals away. Fallen angels flew out of the bowels of the earth like bats from a cave. It was too much – Auroran had to look away. Menkib sat on the floor and covered his face. The cries of the multitudes were overwhelming.

Auroran knew that if his heart ached as it did, how much more the heart of God. *Why,* he wondered, *would God create man and then destroy him? So much rebellion, so much grief, and now mankind had perished. What about the fallen one? Would they be restored or destroyed? Was the war finally over? Where was his brother?* Auroran's thoughts seemed to go everywhere at once.

Without Excuse
Chapter Sixty-Eight

Angels continued to flood into the amphitheater. The arena was abuzz with question after question: "What is happening? Where are the inhabitants? What happened to the fallen ones?"

At the peak of confusion, *Tyl,* the angel from the Temple, stepped forward and asked for silence:

"The God of Heaven and earth has sent me to make an announcement so that all may know that these men are an example to those who afterward might choose to follow ungodly ways. The LORD has said, 'I will destroy man whom I have created from the face of the earth, both man and beast, creeping things and birds of the air, for I am sorry that I made them.'" Tyl continued: "Let it be understood that since the creation of the world His invisible attributes have always been clearly seen, being understood by the things that are made, even His eternal power and Godhead, so that man is without excuse."

"Therefore, God emptied the storehouses of the waters of the deep on the earth destroying every living thing except for one man, Noah, a just man, perfect in his generations. This man Noah found grace in the eyes of the LORD. Therefore God made provisions for Noah and his family saying, 'The end of all flesh has come before Me, make for yourself an ark; you shall bring two of every *sort* of living thing into the ark, to keep *them* alive with you; they shall be male and female – then everything that is left on the earth shall die.'"

Even as Tyl spoke, *Corona* revealed flash floods rushing over the face of the earth, sheets of rain plummeting, and torrents gushing violently. The skies were black with rebels.

Tyl continued: "From the time of creation until God gave the commandment for Noah to build the ark are One thousand, five hundred and thirty six man-years. Noah finished building the ark in One hundred and twenty man-years, for God declared 'My Spirit shall not strive with man forever. He is indeed flesh; yet his days shall be One hundred and twenty years.' Still men did not repent, choosing to live according to their own will, and their women who produced the fruit of ungodliness."

The Temple angel turned to *Corona* to point to a tiny image floating, rising and falling on the surface of rolling waves and flood waters.

"God has ordained on this very day that Noah and Noah's sons – Shem, Ham, and Japheth, and their wives, and Noah's wife, are in the ark – eight souls in all, and the LORD shut them in with the animals. On the day they were shut in, all the fountains of the great deep were broken up and the windows of Heaven opened."

Tyl lifted his hands and declared:

"Holy and exalted is our God. Zealous in His righteousness, perfect in

His glory, His judgments are right and true. Beside Him there is no other! You are worthy, O Lord, to receive glory and honor and power, for You created all things, and by Your will they exist. The LORD knows all the ways of the righteous, but the ways of the ungodly shall perish."

Tyl disappeared. Aside from Tyl, not a single angel left the arena of the amphitheater. Lightening, thunder, and storms prevailed as the ark bobbed up and down in a pitchy sea of darkness and utter isolation. The rebels had no where to land and no where to go.

It was evident to Auroran the unnatural offspring of rebel angels were entirely wiped out. Man would thereafter be able to start over with a clean blood line through Noah and his family.

Memories
Chapter Sixty Nine

The flood left Auroran empty. He sat on the veranda reminiscing, examining his thoughts one at a time as though each one was a part in a parade passing by.

Some one thousand, five hundred and thirty six man-years had passed since the angels sat in the amphitheater seeing something new and wonderful at God's creation. He and Borealis were inseparable then. He smiled as he remembered how Acamar, their new friend, followed them into the vault to look at the earth in the ages to come. They gazed in awe at an earth divided. *Ironically, "the age to come" has arrived and it doesn't look so wonderful,* Auroran groaned. *Lucifer is now Satán and Acamar is now Akkamar.*

According to D'shubba, even as the hosts of angels were gathering in the amphitheater during the flooding of the earth, Satán and his hierarchy had entered the *Honorarium* and stolen the tome *The Physics of the Souls of Men*, unaware the earth was being flooded. How shocked they must have been when they returned to the earth.

How frustrated Satán must be after chasing so many genealogies, for only Noah and his family were left, a total of eight people.

Borealis was still missing. He could not even find a rumor of his whereabouts.

Wearied, Auroran stood as his thoughts tumbled together into a temporary oblivion.

He had an appointment to meet Menkib and wanted to leave early. Menkib did not look well these days. Auroran planned his trip carefully before leaving. He wanted to allow enough time to walk through Wilon and Raki'a where he could see the pillared Arches of Heaven and gaze upon their glory.

As he began his walk, he felt reinvigorated. The Path of Life ended at the outskirts of Ma'on. After some time, the Arches of Heaven came into view. Tall and narrow, like pillared gazebos, the sculpted arches dotted the landscape. They were but one of the many wonders of heaven. A multitude of dimensions converged within each arch creating the translucent sheen of a multicolored pearl. Clouds of angels floated in and out creating a hazy aura around their vibrant splendor.

The Fifth Great Arch had much to do with mankind and, in particular, Enoch. He did not understand this, but did not need to.

Auroran chose a straight and narrow path, away from the Arches of Heaven, to stay focused on the path leading into the Forest of Wisdom. The rich aroma of trees perfumed the forest, filling Auroran with a new sense of strength and vigor. In the cool breeze, he decided to sit a while on a log near a small slope. Behind him a waterfall of words trickled, rippled down, cascading over cold, hard rocks of solid sounds. The pond at the bottom collected the deep and unsearchable pools of living Words. Trapped by an eddy, the Words swirled into paragraphs, revealing truths, some Auroran understood and others remained a mystery.

Auroran looked up. Trees, aloof and upright, reached upward toward the expanse of the higher heavens. Auroran decided it was time to continue; he picked out a few stones of prudence, smooth and white, to carry with him. Every step was enjoyable as he emerged from the forest to walk around the mountain of God and down to the bridge to *Makon* where he caught sight of Menkib in the distance.

"Greetings, my friend!" Auroran cried out.

Menkib signaled him to meet behind the storehouses.

Auroran greeted him again. "A welcome and much needed visit, eh?"

Menkib responded, but not with the same enthusiasm. "Greetings to you, Auroran."

The two angels sat behind the empty storehouses in privacy and isolation. "What is it, Menkib? I see you need to speak your mind."

Menkib finally spoke out, "Why would a holy and just God allow such a catastrophe to take place that wreaks so much suffering?" Menkib blurted. "God *knew* all this would come to pass even before He created it! Hades is a land as dark as darkness itself, the shadow of death, without order, where even light is darkness that overflows with the souls of the dead doomed to perdition for all eternity! When I consider these reflections, I ask myself: Why does God so completely ruin His creatures and render them so miserable, so without help, so abandoned that it hardly seems rational to believe in a God of justice?"

"But God is not the one who has done all this," Auroran lamented.

"Have you been to Hades?" Menkib moaned.

"No, my friend, I do not care to visit such a place." Auroran was shocked at Menkib's outburst, but he held his silence in order to allow Menkib the freedom to express himself and empty his thoughts. Auroran saw the torment written within the knitted brow of Menkib's face. Only when his friend had finished did he take his time to respond. "I have no answer for you, Menkib, but I trust the Almighty. He will make everything beautiful in its time."

"No, Auroran. There is no hope. God cannot and will not compromise with *Sin*. If you were to ask me, 'Can God make a giraffe into a lion?' I would answer, 'Of course!' Or if you were to say, 'Can God clear the table of this universe and bring in another?' I would agree wholeheartedly He could. But who can bring a clean *thing* out of an unclean thing? Not even God can compromise when it comes to sin. Can you tell me this is not so?"

"You are right," Auroran said. "It is so, Menkib. But we do not understand the ways of God. He is the Almighty. His authority is beyond challenge. He is sovereign and His ways are just. Destruction was made for the wicked, and disaster for the workers of iniquity."

"But it *can* be challenged, Auroran! Satán has promised a restoration, a time of a global government where all men will live in peace. If enough angels follow him, God's authority can be superseded."

"Are you recruiting me, Menkib?" Auroran scowled.

"No, Auroran, no.... I am speaking to a friend who, I hope, understands my turmoil. You can clearly see I am looking for an answer, *any one* answer that may make sense! I need words to cool my heated heart."

"So you have not rebelled, Menkib?"

"I have signed no contract with Satán, but my heart rages. God sits on His throne high in His Temple unscathed while mankind is destroyed – while angels rebel –while eternal souls are doomed forever. He gives no explanations, nor does He defend his actions."

"Nor should He, Menkib! He is the Lord God Almighty who created all things in earth and in Heaven for his pleasure."

"That's what I mean, Auroran, for *His* pleasure." Menkib held his head in his hands as though in a vice grip.

"God does not take pleasure in the death of the wicked, but He pleads with men to repent. Let me ask you this, Menkib." Auroran touched his friend's shoulder. "What would God have to do to earn your trust?"

"To earn *my* trust?" Menkib jerked forward to give Auroran his answer. "A skin for a skin! He would have to put *His* suffering on the table. Let Him suffer like these men." Menkib pounded his fist. "Let *His* Soul see Hades!" His eyes fulgurated strangely, with the look of an executioner. He jumped up and left at the speed of light.

Auroran wasn't given a chance to say another word. *No, Menkib! Don't do it!*

A Proper Order
Chapter Seventy

Zuben sought out Menkib who had retreated into solitude after the flood. After much searching, he found him sitting with his head in his hands looking out over the Sea of Nothingness on the far side of Heaven. "You have been a faithful warrior, Menkib, and I have been proud to have you under my command, but I can see this flood has affected you tremendously."

"It has been a difficult thing. Hades was one thing, but now the flood?"

"Is it so difficult to trust God, Menkib?" Zuben asked earnestly.

"God has all the Power, all the Glory, and all for ... for *what?*" Menkib answered still staring into the Sea of Nothingness. "Why would God create men who are destined for Hades?" Menkib murmured.

"A person destined for Hades has not been predestined by God. This is false. People choose to go there rather than submit their lives to God. They have absolute free will. They are punished to the degree of evil they commit in their life. This is why God allows people to make their own choices. Angels also have free will. Should God not have created angels?"

"What makes you think men can escape death and Hades, Zuben?" Menkib argued. "God has said nothing of a plan for this."

"Enoch," Zuben answered, pointing toward the City of God. He then paused a moment before continuing. "Enoch is God's visible pledge of an undisclosed plan."

Menkib's countenance brightened. "Oh! But how? How can God do this?"

"God isn't finished yet, Menkib. We must trust." Zuben smiled. "Even God's wrath is a sign of His Love."

Menkib frowned. "That does not make sense, Zuben."

"If men chose to go to Hades rather than submit to God," Zuben implored, "think how much worse it would be if they were allowed to continue in their evil ways, not only on earth, but in their eternal destiny. God's grace must have a limit. If it did not, think of how man's society would be – think of what it *has* been."

Menkib shuddered. *Zuben had a point. Prior to the flood, he had complained that God was doing nothing. Now that God took action he was angry, not at the men who had refused God, not at Satán and his angels, but at God. He saw now how Satán's actions had infiltrated Heaven and spread confusion once again.* "I see you are right, Zuben. I think I can see things in their proper order."

Zuben stayed with his friend, hoping somehow he had helped. They sat and talked about many things until Zuben had to leave to return to his duties.

Rest - Comfort
Chapter Seventy-One

Noah stood looking through the small window at the top of the ark. A warm wind blew through the window and warmed him. He was still grieving for those who had perished in the flood.

Noah stroked his beard as he reminisced about his father and mother who had named him Noah, meaning Rest, Comfort, Sigh, or Relief. He and his family descended from the lineage of Seth, the brother of Cain. Perhaps now, he thought, there might be rest. His father had died five years before the flood but his grandfather, Methuselah perished the same year as the flood. Noah thought the meaning of his grandfather's name odd since it meant "His death shall bring," and that he died just before the rains. Noah was grateful his great grandfather, Enoch the teacher, had been taken by God without seeing death and without witnessing this great devastation.

Noah breathed deeply. He thought about the taunting of his neighbors as he built the ark. Never before had anyone seen rain or knew what rain was. The earth had been enclosed in an ice canopy and a mist came up from the chambers under the earth. He could still remember the taunting, "Nothing has changed since the beginning of our father Adam."

He looked at the marks slashed in the wood by the window for each day they had been in the ark. Noah took a piece of metal and added another slash to the one hundred and forty nine marks. Now there were one hundred and fifty marks since God had closed the door to the ark and sealed them in. He thought of the irony that the entire ark was sealed with a pitch called "kopher" meaning "atonement."

For the first forty days and nights they heard nothing but thunder and the pounding of wind and rain. The ark tossed every which way amid the tribulation of turbulence while enveloped in abysmal darkness. It reminded him of creation; how the earth was without form, and void; and darkness was on the face of the deep. And the Spirit of God hovered over the face of the waters.

During those chaotic, terrifying, dark forty days the animals also cried out in distress. He tied to comfort his family by telling them that if God had put them in the ark, He would not allow the ark to be lost to the elements; therefore, they had nothing to fear.

It seemed to Noah that the violent darkness and rains were so severe, they pierced the spirit world. Even though he did not see dark principalities, he knew they were in the skies overhead; but he also knew both he and his family were protected by the ark. It was as though they were encapsulated in a womb protecting them from the influences of an outer world.

Noah continued to look out the window at the still waters and his spirit rose, *today was a new day!* When he woke that morning to a sun beam shooting across the ceiling of the ark, he knew this was a new beginning. He felt the ark bump and rock just slightly. He realized the ark was caught between large rocks on a piece of land. The waters had subsided enough for the ark to touch upon a tiny island in the middle of an endless ocean.

As he gazed upon the waters he heard bleating, trumpeting, roaring, cooing, clucking, barking, snorting and other animal noises in the background. Then he heard his wife, Naamah calling him, "Father! These boards holding the lions are broken and their hay is falling about!" Noah sighed.

Both he and his wife's fathers had the same name: Lamech, although his father was a descendent of Seth and Naamah's father was a descendent of Cain, both fathers were adamant their children would have a brighter, easier future.

He girded his loins by pulling the skirt of his robe from the back to the front and up to his waist where he secured it. There was much work to be done and he needed to be unencumbered to do it. He scratched the head of the giraffe nuzzling him before heading down into the bowels of the ship where the animals were waiting impatiently.

Captured
Chapter Seventy-Two

As Noah fed the animals, rebel angels continued to fly overhead, they were starving having nothing to eat and no light to sustain them. Flying above the waters demanded much energy draining each one of his small reserves.

When the rebels saw the ark floating on the waters, they flocked like blackbirds to rest on its hull. As though it were a carcass, they pushed and shoved trying their best to rest before being shoved off by another rebel. Others tried to save their energy by soaring in circles instead of fighting.

As rebels circled endlessly, a raven went to and fro over the face of the waters searching for land.

When Noah opened the ark's tiny window; an emaciated angel tried to crawl through it but could not fit. He was soon pulled loose by another starving angel and tossed aside, each one trying to get a piece of Noah's hue.

One by one the depleted rebels fell into the waters, floating helplessly and powerlessly upon its surface.

Zuben, Menkib, and troops of other warrior angels were then dispatched from heaven to capture the rebels who had nowhere to hide, nothing to fight with, and no energy with which to fight.

The warrior angels found it easy to pluck them out of the air and drag them from the buoyant waters. As they were rounded up they were bound in shackles of darkness and cast into the bottomless pit reserved for their day of judgment.

After the roundup Zuben and Menkib looked for Satán and his hierarchy, but they were nowhere to be found.

Satán and the five watched from afar having just returned from their surreptitious activities in heaven. Upon finding and taking Jo'el's books undetected, they decided to stay in heaven and celebrate their triumph by soaking in the Glory of God which pervaded the heavens until ready to return to earth revived and refreshed.

They weren't prepared for their shock upon returning, seeing the earth swallowed up in a flood while warrior angels drug the bodies of rebels from an endless ocean of water. There was no earth.

He and his hierarchy alone had the energy to escape their captures.

Patience
Chapter Seventy-Three

Day after day slash marks were added alongside the ark's window, increasing by yet another one hundred and twenty. Noah, with Naamah at his side, concluded it was now two hundred and seventy days since the torrents began.

The ark had permanently settled. No longer did they feel afloat, but had to adjust to the stability under their feet.

Each one took turns peering through the window; encouraged by spotting islands dotting the ocean's landscape.

"Let's open the door," Naamah encouraged Noah. But the time was not yet right.

"Patience," Noah reassured them. "Patience, wait upon the Lord."

A Dove
Chapter Seventy-Four

After adding another thirty slashes by the window, Noah sent out a dove instead of a raven; but it also returned. Even Noah's patience was wavering. He waited only another seven days before sending it out again. This time it returned and landed on him having plucked an olive leaf, holding the twig in its beak.

Plucked, Noah smiled, *just as God had plucked Enoch taking him to heaven. Now, after this tribulation of a flood, the Spirit of God sat on him extending an olive branch of peace. Doves only land on something clean to let them know the judgment is over.*

Noah, Naamah, their three sons and their son's wives gloried in their new beginning. The waters had abated from the earth but it was another sixty days before they were able to emerge from the ark into a colorful sun drenched sky.

Yes, Noah sighed, *the darkness had abated.*

Surprised
Chapter Seventy-Five

"My friend!" D'shubba hailed Auroran, grinning. "Come. Let's go to the arena."

"What news?" Auroran asked. "Can any good thing come from the arena?"

"This time good tidings, my friend," D'shubba smiling broadly as he hurried Auroran along. "Trust me, you will see."

"Why shouldn't I be suspicious when I see a smile on your face as we are paying a visit to the arena? These are incongruous." Auroran dug his heels in as D'shubba pulled him along.

When D'shubba arrived with Auroran in tow, Zuben was waiting, dressed in his finest military regalia. Zuben led them through the back hallways behind the arena's stage and onto the back of the stage. They stood behind thick, heavy tapestries. D'shubba and Zuben both waited in silence bearing peculiar grins. Auroran heard a strange, hushed noise coming from the other side of the tapestries where he once sat in the audience when God created mankind. After an a short but uncomfortable span of time, the curtains opened revealing Auroran in the center of the stage looking out into an audience of angels erupting into applause. A confetti of twinkling stars streamed into the audience and onto the stage, swirling downward, landing haphazardly wherever they fell.

"Wh- what is this?" Auroran turned to his friends at the side of the stage.

"We have a surprise for you," D'shubba and Zuben replied in unison walking onstage to join him. "Look!" They pointed to the auditorium filled with heavenly hosts. But the overflowing crowd of angels did not clarify Auroran's confusion, it only added to it, until, from among the masses, one angel rose and walked toward the front.

The auditorium of angels threw flowers at the feet of Borealis as he walked forward grinning and waving. The choir sang *God is Victorious, Ancient of Days.*

Auroran couldn't believe his eyes. It was Borealis! In *full* military attire! When Borealis approached, Auroran choked on his tears as he hugged his brother.

Borealis grinned from ear to ear.

Zuben stepped in. "You are just in time to see your brother honored, Auroran."

"Honored?" Auroran couldn't catch up.

Zuben had Borealis step forward as he placed a glistening wreath of tiny stars on Borealis' head creating a halo lighting up an already effervescent face. "In appreciation of your sacrifice in the LORD's service, I, Zuben, commander of the LORD's army, am hereby authorized to promote you to the position of Bene-angel." He then proceeded to add the Bene-angel pin to Borealis' armband.

"Bene-Angel!" Auroran gasped, "Bene-Angels are free to choose their own assignments – or have no assignment at all." Auroran stood aghast through the jubilant coronation.

"I think someone had better tell Auroran what has taken place before he loses his footing." D'shubba laughed.

"Yes, please, someone tell me!" Auroran pleaded, looking around, dazed. "Borealis! What is this about?"

Zuben answered: "It was Borealis who rode the comet that crashed into the earth on assignment from the Almighty God."

"He fought off the princes of the air single-handedly in order to return to the heavens!" D'shubba beamed.

"Borealis," Auroran stuttered, "I thought...."

"Yes," Zuben replied. "I knew what you thought, but I couldn't tell you about his undercover assignments. I couldn't tell anyone. I'm sorry, Auroran. I know how you have suffered. Because of this, I have the authority to present you with this medallion of patience and endurance." Zuben also pinned Auroran as angels cheered.

Outside the amphitheater, a procession waited to take Borealis and Auroran to The Temple where they would be received into the presence of the Almighty.

Catching Up
Chapter Seventy-Six

As they rode to the temple, Auroran and Borealis had time to catch up.

Borealis explained the events of the recent past. "That's right," Borealis admitted to his brother. "I made a copy of your key to the bottomless pit as directed by the Lord."

"Tell me once again," Auroran said, still trying to figure it out. "By agreeing to meet with Satán, you were shown the layout of his cavern and his war room? But why did you goad Satán into taking the key and throwing you into the bottomless pit?"

"Since Satán was sure I couldn't escape, neither he nor his hierarchy would be suspicious I was crawling around in their caverns. They would have no need to keep track of me and would not be looking for me. The bottomless pit has a shaft going through the middle of Hades where Satán has his headquarters."

"What about Hades?" Auroran prodded. "What's it like?"

"It's a cave located in the bowels of the earth. It's like walking through the mouth of a great fish with stalactites and stalagmites on the top and bottom-like the teeth of a fish. The entrance is large, but the deeper you get the more narrow it becomes, then it is suffocating and you feel as though you are being eaten alive. Once you are inside, it takes on a strange glow. In its middle is the shaft of the bottomless pit where Satán's angels threw me in; like a man being thrown into a furnace."

"Once you were rescued from the bottomless pit, then you had access to the *River of the Living*?" Auroran asked.

"That's right. I had to hide my angelic light to keep from being discovered. I snatched Lucifer's cape from the door to his war room. Then I crawled through his cavern, hiding from his armies, burrowing down the cavern's tunnel to the River of the Living. Then, as directed by the LORD I was given instructions to retrieve Enoch's soul and take it to heaven where God glorified Enoch's body - reuniting body and soul here in the heavens. It's still hard to believe the plan succeeded." Borealis smiled.

"What was it like holding a man's soul in your hands?" Eager for answers, a curious Auroran riddled his brother with questions.

"Men's souls look like a froth swirling in dirty water, except most of the souls are stiff. They stick together, engorged and bloated with pride. Enoch's soul was still soft and pliable although other souls felt hardened and thick. Light could not penetrate the thickened souls. Still -," Borealis paused in thought, "I noticed something odd; when my light shone into Enoch's soul, the light seemed to move into other souls through his membrane. I think righteous men have the ability to spread light to other men."

"But Paradise is on the other side of the *River of the Living*. Why didn't you go through Paradise to retrieve Enoch's soul?" Before waiting for an answer, Auroran continued: "How did you manage to separate Enoch's soul from the rest of the souls without damaging it?"

"It's impossible to cross the *River of the Living*," Borealis replied. "If I had gone through Paradise, we wouldn't have the layout of Satán's headquarters. That was the primary directive. As for Enoch's soul, separating it from the froth was fairly easy. I had a Soul Catcher. I reached into the river and gently pulled on the soul until it was released from the froth without damage. I was able to maintain its shape."

"Could you see Paradise?"

Auroran's questions were limitless, but Borealis enjoyed sharing his adventure with his brother because it gave him a chance to relive the excitement. "Everything was dark in Hades, but across the river it looked like a perpetual sunrise, and I knew the light came from Paradise. While I retrieved Enoch's soul, I tried my best to see Paradise but, like I said, everything was dark. I did see some beautiful colored globes, shining in a forest across from the river on the edge of Paradise."

"But the bottomless pit!" Auroran shuddered. "Was it necessary to accept being thrown into the bottomless pit?"

"It was the only way to get the layout of Satán's headquarters. It was a radical plan, but it worked. You are right about the suffering. I will tell you the truth; I don't believe I could accept such an assignment again." Borealis' voice trailed off.

"Who rescued you? Was it Zuben? Menkib?"

"No, they escorted me to Hades, taking a break from guarding the entrance to the Garden of Eden, but they had to leave before rebel angels saw them," Borealis crossed his brows. "It was another angel, an unknown angel sent by the LORD. It was He who reached in and pulled me out of the pit. If Zuben or Menkib had tried to reach in, they would have been sucked in by the pit."

Auroran then remembered Menkib mentioning Hades. He should have realized back then that Menkib had been to Hades. Auroran returned to questioning his brother. "But you do not know the angel who rescued you?" Auroran asked, pondering.

"No." Borealis tried to recollect anything that might give him a clue. "No ... I can't remember anything that would help me identify him. But I'm sure he will be revealed in his own time."

"So many mysteries," Auroran murmured.

"I never felt such relief as when I was pulled from that pit."

"I can't believe I doubted you." Auroran shook his head. "Had I not doubted you, I might have been able to help you in some way."

"You were not to know," Borealis said, comforting his brother with his words. "It wouldn't have been beneficial to anyone."

"So you were working undercover for the Lord all this time?"

"Yes, up to and including bringing the comet to earth. For all I know, Satán still thinks I'm in the bottomless pit."

"And Satán still has the copy of its key. In the arena we watched the flood and the harrowing darkness of the storm. We saw rebel angels swarming above the flood." Auroran took a deep breath. "You have lived a life of much danger, my brother." Auroran sat amazed, admiring his brother.

Borealis nodded, smiled. "It's how God created me."

"Yes, I understand now." Auroran sat back, stupefied. "Angels may be more like men than I realized."

"What do you mean?" Borealis asked

"We refuse to see what we don't want to believe. I see now that you, my brother, are greater than I."

End of Volume One

One Angel's Opinion
Auroran's Declaration: "You, my brother, are greater than I."

A NOTE FROM THE AUTHOR

While it is enjoyable to speculate on what heaven is like, based on scripture - scriptural truths must be taken seriously.

I would be remiss not to share this good news: God has provided a cure for sin. The Son of God came down from heaven to redeem men and women from the slave market of sin by shedding his own sinless blood. He was buried, and on the third day he rose from the dead.

"This is love, not that we loved God, but that He loved us and sent His Son to be the settlement for our sins. For God so loved (everyone in) the world that He gave His (one and) only begotten Son, that whoever believes in Him should not perish but have everlasting life. He who believes in Him is not condemned; but he who does not believe is condemned already, because he has not believed in the name (the identity, the purpose, the validity) of the only begotten (raised from the dead) Son of God." 1 John 4:10 John 3:16-18 NKJV

Notice the word: ONLY. There is ONLY one cure.

Watch for the release of upcoming Volumes of One Angel's Opinion.

Questions (Answers on Following Pages):
One Angel's Opinion and Scriptural Truths:

1. Were angels present at creation?
2. I always thought heaven was a peaceful place?
3. Don't angels know everything?
4. Isn't the giving of rewards and promotions of positions unspiritual?
5. Were angels, in the book One Angel's Opinion, showing off their positions with medallions and promotions?
6. Isn't it wrong to use the imagination to write about angels and heaven?
7. Is fiction evil?
8. How does anyone know what happened before the creation?
9. What does the usage of being "set apart" mean in One Angel's Opinion?
10. Is God being deceitful when sending Borealis as a spy?
11. Is it wrong to be deceptive with evil?
12. Should a believer hide from evil?
13. What's the difference between sin and evil?
14. Why does the book have angel's sleeping (resting)?
15. Are there alternate realities?
16. Are Atiks fairies? Are Lucent angels aliens?
17. Are rumors gossip?
18. Is Kasdaye using magic in heaven when he waves his hands and sparkles appear?
19. Is Beth, the daughter of Adam in scripture?
20. Did Methuselah really die the same year as the flood?
21. Do the two keys named, "Decided and Done" have any scriptural reference?
22. What does imbroglio mean? Isn't there an easier word for more people to understand?
23. Would God allow incest?
24. Comments on the age of the earth.
25. Are dimensions from God?
26. Why is hail being stored?
27. Isn't "I AM" the name of God and not Satán when he says "I AM" in his cavern?

28. Are the body and the soul different entities?

29. Isn't God lying when he doesn't tell the angels everything?

30. Why did Lamech ask if God could forgive him seventy-fold?

31. Isn't man's "hue" a new age concept, like an aura?

32. What are the frogs in the bottomless pit?

33. What is the basis for the broken compass Satán hands to his hierarchy?

34. Are there really an angel of fire and an angel of water?

35. Why did God destroy the earth and everything in it? Was it because of man's polluted DNA when fallen angels had relations with the daughters of men, or because mankind was violent?

36. Was Naamah in Genesis 4:22 really the wife of Noah?

37. Is there a "Mount of the Congregation" in scripture?

38. Did Lucifer walk among the "stones of fire" on the holy mountain of God?

39. Where did the concept of capturing rebel angels and putting them in Hell come from?

40. Where did the concept of "Lies" being like poisonous darts/ninja spikes/weapons originate?

41. Is the book, One Angel's Opinion, comparing Enoch and Noah with the rapture and the tribulation?

42. What is the meaning in One Angel's Opinion, of God's pronouncement of One Hundred and Twenty years for men at the time of the flood? "My Spirit shall not strive with man forever. He is indeed flesh; yet his days shall be One Hundred and Twenty years."

43. Why is man's rest in the thirteenth dimension? Why is the spiritual world in the eleventh dimension?

44. Zuben is called a "strong angel." Does scripture refer to some angels as being "strong?"

45. In Chapter One the angels fall down and worship God saying "Holy, holy, holy." What is your opinion on why they say holy three times?

46. What is the purpose for writing a book like this?

47. God made a Covenant, a pact, with man at the beginning of the book. Is there a scriptural reference for this?

48. Abel's name means "whiff or breeze," doesn't it also mean "unnecessary?"

49. The Title indicates "One Angel's Opinion, Auroran's Declaration" is Volume One. Are there more volumes to come? Is this the beginning of a series?

1. Were angels present at creation?

According to Job 38:4-7 they were: "Where were you when I laid the foundations of the earth? Tell Me, if you have understanding. Who determined its measurements? Surely you know! Or who stretched the line upon it? To what were its foundations fastened? Or who laid its cornerstone, When the morning stars sang together, And all the sons of God shouted for joy?" NKJV

2. I always thought heaven was a peaceful place?

Revelation 12:7
And war broke out in heaven: Michael and his angels fought with the dragon; and the dragon and his angels fought,

3. Don't angels know everything?

Angels are not God. Scripture says angels desire to look into the things that are revealed to men.

"His (God's) intent was that now, through the church, the manifold wisdom of God should be made known (revealed) to the rulers and authorities in the heavenly realms," Ephesians 3:10.

"To them it was revealed that, not to themselves, but to us they were ministering the things which now have been reported to you through those who have preached the gospel to you by the Holy Spirit sent from heaven—things which angels desire to look into." 1 Peter 1:12

Likewise, angels would not have fallen if they did not question God.

4. Isn't the giving of rewards and promotions of positions unspiritual?

"The laborer is worthy of his reward." 1 Timothy 5:18 NKJV

There are two unalterable truths in scripture:
>The first is:
>>Indeed, under the law almost everything is purified with blood, and without the shedding of blood there is no forgiveness of sins. Hebrews 9:22 ESV

>And the second is:
>>But without faith it is impossible to please Him, for he who comes to God must believe that He is, and that He is a rewarder of those who diligently seek Him. Hebrews 11:6 NKJV

Therefore; it is critical to believe in rewards.

5. Were angels, in the book One Angel's Opinion, showing off their positions with medallions and promotions?

No. Remember- God is a God of reward. God's kingdom is not communistic.

However; no one is shunned or looked down upon or valued less because of their rewards. Rewards are synonymous with the taking on of more responsibility.

Psalm 58:11 So that men will say, "Surely there is <u>a reward</u> for the righteous; Surely He is God who judges in the earth." NKJV

Isaiah 62:11 [11] Indeed the Lord has proclaimed to the end of the world: "Say to the daughter of Zion, 'Surely your salvation is coming; Behold, <u>His reward</u> *is* with Him, And His work before Him.'" NKJV

Matthew 5:12 Rejoice and be exceedingly glad, for great is your <u>reward</u> in heaven, NKJV

Hebrews 11:6 "But without faith it is impossible to please Him, for he who comes to God must believe that He is, and that He is a <u>rewarder</u> of those who diligently seek Him." NKJV

1 Corinthians 9:24 "[Striving for a Crown] Do you not know that those who run in a race all run, but one receives the prize? Run in such a way that you may obtain it." (Crowns of Life, crowns of Glory, crowns of Righteousness, etc. All these crowns are rewards mentioned in scripture.)

6. Isn't it wrong to use the imagination to write about angels and heaven?

The imagination is a necessary part of the soul. Man cannot live without the imagination any more than he can live without a stomach. Without imagination there are no dreams, no motivation, and no life.

People become lost without imagination. If someone asks how to drive to a house and they are given directions, it is the imagination that draws a map in the mind so that the person is able to get there.

The imagination is neither good or bad it simply "is." We, as fallen men, have the choice to use our imagination for good or evil. The imagination is like a match: it can light a fire and warm the house or it can burn the house to the ground. The imagination can be used to write wonderful books or it can be used to delve into porn.

When God destroyed the earth, it was when the imagination of men had become evil continually.

> And God saw that the wickedness of man was great in the earth, and that every imagination of the thoughts of his heart was only evil continually. Genesis 6:5 KJV

7. Is fiction evil?

Fiction, like the imagination, can be used for good or for evil. Parables, songs, and poetry all are fiction even if they have some or a lot of truth to them. A parable by definition is a story that illustrates God-given truths. The range of meaning of the term "parable" in the New Testament closely parallels that of the Hebrew term "masal" in the Old Testament and related Hebrew literature. As well as referring to narrative parables, the term identifies similitudes (Matt 13:33; B. Pes. 49a), allegories (Ezek 17:2 ; 24:3; Matthew 13:18,24 & 36), proverbs (Proverbs 1:1 Proverbs 1:6 ; Mark 3:23), riddles (Psalm 78:2 ; Mark 7:17), and symbols or types (Heb 9:9 ; B. Sanh. 92b).

One Angel's Opinion is a window through which a larger reality is depicted illustrating aspects of the kingdom of God, the reign of God in people's hearts, and the realm of God's sovereignty.

8. How does anyone know what happened before the creation?

> Acts 2:22-24 NASB
> Jesus the Nazarene, a man attested to you by God with miracles and wonders and signs which God performed through Him in your midst, just as you yourselves know—this Man, delivered over by the <u>predetermined plan and foreknowledge of God</u>, you nailed to a cross by the hands of godless men and put Him to death. But God raised Him up again, putting an end to the agony of death, since it was impossible for Him to be held in its power.

> Revelation 13:8 NKJV
> All who dwell on the earth will worship him, whose names have not been written in the Book of Life of the Lamb slain <u>from the foundation of the world.</u>

> 1 Corinthians 2:7 NKJV
> But we speak the wisdom of God in a mystery, the hidden wisdom which God ordained <u>before the ages for our glory,</u>

9. What does the usage of being "set apart" mean in One Angel's Opinion?

It means fulfilling an assignment given by God.

The Spirit leads us through this mine field. Each person is led differently. We must let the Spirit lead us in the direction He wants us to go just as God led Abraham to leave Ur and go to Canaan. God leads some to feast and others to fast. God leads some into politics, others to music, others to write. (We fall into dangerous pits of error if we tell others how to serve or praise God.) There is only one God and only one way to God but there are many gifts and many uses for our gifts.

> Matthew 9:14 "Then the disciples of John came to Him, saying, "Why do we and the Pharisees fast often, but Your disciples do not fast?"

> Matthew 11:16-19 "But to what shall I liken this generation? It is like children sitting in the marketplaces and calling to their companions, and saying: 'We played the flute for you, And you did not dance; We mourned to you, And you did not lament.' For John came neither eating nor drinking, and they say, 'He has a demon.' The Son of Man came eating and drinking, and they say, 'Look, a glutton and a winebibber, a friend of tax collectors and sinners!'"

In other words, God sends some to play the flute and others to lament so that any may be brought to God.

> 1 Corinthians 9:19-22 "For though I am free from all men, I have made myself a servant to all, that I might win the more; and to the Jews I became as a Jew, that I might win Jews; to those who are under the law, as under the law, that I might win those who are under the law; to those who are without law, as without law (not being without law toward God, but under law toward Christ), that I might win those who are without law; to the weak I became as weak, that I might win the weak. I have become all things to all men that I might by all means save some."

10. Is God being deceitful when sending Borealis as a spy?

God sent spies to spy out the Promised Land. God sent spies to Jericho. One of the spies, Salmon, married Rahab the harlot and they are honored by being part of the royal lineage of Jesus.

Rahab lied to save the spies when the King of Jericho sent for her and God blessed her for this:

> The king of Jericho was told, "Look, some of the Israelites have come here tonight to spy out the land." So the king of Jericho sent this message to Rahab: "Bring out the men who came to you and entered your house, because they have come to spy out the whole land." But the woman had taken the two men and hidden them. She said, "Yes, the men came to me, but I did not know where they had come from. At dusk, when it was time to close the city gate, they left. I don't know which way they went. Go after them quickly. You may catch up with them." (But she had taken them up to the roof and hidden them under the stalks of flax she had laid out on the roof.) So the men set out in pursuit of the spies on the road that leads to the fords of the Jordan, and as soon as the pursuers had gone out, the gate was shut.

11. Is it wrong to be deceptive with evil?

Was it wrong for people to hide Jews during the holocaust and lie to the Nazis? Jesus told his disciples to be as crafty as the serpent but as innocent as the dove. Innocence comes from the motivations of the heart. For the pure in heart all things are pure.

> Titus 1:15 "Unto the pure all things are pure: but unto them that are defiled and unbelieving is nothing pure; but even their mind and conscience is defiled." NKJV

12. Should a believer hide from evil?

There comes a time when it is appropriate.

> John 8:59 "Then took they up stones to cast at him: <u>but Jesus hid himself</u>, and went out of the temple, going through the midst of them, and so passed by." NKJV

13. What's the difference between sin and evil?

Sin is doing wrong. Evil is deliberately refusing to accept God's character and plan even when confronted with His truths.

14. Why does the book have angel's sleeping (resting)?

God did not need to rest but He rested on the seventh day and declared it holy. God even gives the land a rest. Heaven itself is a place of rest (paradise=rest) even though Lucifer polluted it with his rebellion. God teaches rest. The millennium is a thousand years of rest.

15. Are there alternate realities?

No, there could be if God had decided it to be so. Only God can see all possible futures and outcomes. His desired Will will be done.

Anyone can count the seeds in an apple, but only God can count all possible apples that will come forever out of one seed. Furthermore; God can see all the "what ifs" that might have happened with that one seed.

16. Are Atiks fairies? Are Lucent angels aliens?

No, Atiks are tiny angels spawned from the imagination of the author as are the Lucents.

Are they mentioned in scripture? No.

Is it wrong to imagine tiny angels or tall white angels? No, as long as truth is told in revealing they are from the imagination of the author and have no association with the evil philosophies of Satán.

With that being said, it is possible for a time to come when we learn aliens may be fallen angels in UFOs. Perhaps relating to the verse below:

> Luke 21:11 ESV
> There will be great earthquakes, and in various places famines and pestilences. And there will be terrors and great signs from heaven.

17. Are rumors gossip?

Rumors aren't necessarily the result of gossip. Gossip is used for the defamation of character. Rumors are the search for truth gathered through unconventional means until the veracity of that information is either confirmed or denounced. This is not to say that fallen angels would not use gossip and rumors to defame character.

18. Is Kasdaye using magic in heaven when he waves his hands and sparkles appear?

>Not at all. God gives special gifts to be used for righteous purposes. However; when an angel rebels, it would make sense he would use his gifts for evil.

>This is the same for men. Men have the option to use their God-given gifts for good or for evil.

19. Is Beth, the daughter of Adam in scripture?

>No. She is added because when Cain went to Nod it was a place of many people. Where did those people come from? This is the book's explanation: From Beth and a fallen angel.

20. Did Methuselah really die the same year as the flood?

>According to Biblical genealogies, the answer is yes.

21. Do the two keys named, "Decided and Done" have any scriptural reference?

>Joseph spoke the following to the Pharaoh after interpreting his dreams:
>>Genesis 41:32 NIV
>>"The reason the dream was given to Pharaoh in <u>two forms</u> is because the matter has been <u>firmly</u> <u>decided</u> by God, and God will <u>do it</u> soon."

>To paraphrase: "It is decided and it is done."

22. What does imbroglio mean? Isn't there an easier word for more people to understand?

>Im·bro·glio noun: - An extremely confused, complicated, or embarrassing situation. Its synonyms include: complicated situation, complication, problem, difficulty, predicament, trouble, confusion, quandary, entanglement, muddle, mess, quagmire, morass, sticky situation.

>The problem with substituting easier words, sometimes they do not express the depth of the intended meaning.

23. Would God allow incest?

>Incest was not taboo at creation. Incest became taboo because of the deterioration of DNA.

At creation, men had clean DNA. Intermarrying would not have resulted in the passing down of inherited diseases to their children's genes.

However, there are other spiritual reasons incest became taboo as seen in the laws given to the Jews.

24. Comments on the age of the earth:

According to science the universe has <u>expanded</u> a million-million times.

And according to science the universe is 15 billion <u>years old</u>.

Dividing 15 billion by a million-million equals .015 years [the ratio for time dilation] ....or six days.

With a calculator: [15 B/(M*M)=.015 years]

15 Billion=15,000,000,000

A Million-Million=One million multiplied by one million, or 1,000,000 times 1,000,000=1,000,000,000,000

Dividing 15 Billion (expansion) by a Million-Million (years) results in .015 yrs

15,000.000.000 / 1,000,000,000,000 = .015 years

365 days/yr times .015= 5.475 days.

If 5.475 days were rounded up to exactly 6 days [.0164 yr instead of .015], then either the universe is just a smidge over 15 billion years old or the universe expanded just a smidge more that a million-million times.

We must be careful not to confirm scripture with science. However; this is simply one explanation of why we can see light from stars billions of years away when genealogies in scripture indicate the world is only thousands of years old.

25. Are dimensions from God?

Dimensions have to be of God. He created everything and they exist. Perhaps you are asking if there are more than the four dimensions we experience: Width, Depth, Height and Time. Other dimensions are evident not only from scripture but from mathematics. This universe exists in no less than eleven dimensions but there is evidence of even more.

When uniting all known forces into one mathematic equation, it demands no less than eleven dimensions to make this universe plausible.

It takes force to cause motion. Some of the forces of which we are currently aware include the natural forces of gravity and magnetism and the contact forces. Each force has its own mathematical formula.

So the question becomes: what formula explains all the forces in the universe? Answer: The one that includes more dimensions than the four of which we are aware, and at least eleven.

26. Why is hail being stored?

The hailstones in God's storage bins refers to Joshua 10:11 "And it came to pass, as they fled from before Israel, and were in the going down to Beth-horon, that the Lord cast down great stones from heaven upon them unto Azekah, and they died: they were more which died with hailstones than they whom the children of Israel slew with the sword."

Also Isaiah 30:30, Ezekiel 13:11 & 13, 38:22, Psalm 18:12-13, Finally: Revelation 16:21 And there fell upon men a great hail out of heaven, every stone about the weight of a talent (75 pounds): and men blasphemed God because of the plague of the hail; for the plague thereof was exceeding great. NKJV

27. Isn't "I AM" the name of God and not Satán?

Satán mimics God by saying "I AM the god of the world…"

And scripture says he is indeed the god of this world –

> 2 Corinthians 4:4 KJV
> "In whom the god of this world hath blinded the minds of them which believe not, lest the light of the glorious gospel of Christ, who is the image of God, should shine unto them."

However, he is not God or even God-like. Although Satán believes he is god, the echo corrects him when it echoes back his demotion to being nothing more than a lowercase "i am."

Satán's existence and our existence give us the right to be "I am," but only God is the great "I AM."

28. Are the body and the soul different entities?

The body dies and returns to the dirt but the soul lives after the death of the body. The soul is made up of men's thoughts and emotions. God does not desire to preserve the body, but Christ died to save man's eternal soul. God will give us new, glorified bodies.

> Matthew 10:28 "And do not fear those who kill the body but cannot kill the soul. But rather fear Him who is able to destroy both soul and body in hell." NKJV

29. Isn't God lying when he doesn't tell the angels everything?

God cannot lie - but neither does He disclose everything. He uses discretion. Furthermore; He never defends Himself. Notice Jesus did not defend Himself against the lies and insults that were hurled at Him. He causes certain people to become blinded to His truths, He speaks in parables, and He hides things, but He does not lie.

There are many secrets and many mysteries He keeps. This concept is critical to understanding God and trusting Him. God told both the apostle Paul and John not to write down certain things that had been revealed to them. There are some truths that people cannot accept, but they belong to God, and there are some truths still to come as yet unrevealed.

The Church during the age of grace is a mystery God kept to Himself until He revealed it to Paul. It's sad to see certain believers treat the writings of Paul as less than relevant. These truths are critical to our understanding of the plan of God for the Bride of Christ - not to be confused with God's further dealings with the nation of Israel, specifically.

30. Why did Lamech ask if God could forgive him seventy-fold?

"If Cain is avenged sevenfold, then I seventy-sevenfold. Can God forgive Lamech seventy times seven?"

This is echoed in Matthew 8:22 when Jesus answered his disciples:

> Matthew 18:21-22 NKJV
> Then Peter came to Him and said, "Lord, how often shall my brother sin against me, and I forgive him? Up to seven times?" Jesus said to him, "I do not say to you, up to seven times, but up to seventy times seven.

It is also in Lamech's mind of the words given to Cain:

Genesis 4:15 NKJV
And the Lord said to him, "Therefore, whoever kills Cain, vengeance shall be taken on <u>him sevenfold</u>." And the Lord set a mark on Cain, lest anyone finding him should kill him.

31. Isn't a man's hue a new age concept, like an aura?

It is similar to men who feed on God's righteousness, except Satán and his angels feed on men's emotions of fear and guilt.

Psalm 37:3
Trust in the Lord, and do good; dwell in the land, and <u>feed on His faithfulness</u>.

Scripture makes it clear Satán merchandizes on the souls of men. Feeding on the emotions of men is symbolic of how Satán uses men for his own desires. Satán plays havoc with the emotions of men.

Nahum 3:16
You have multiplied your merchants more than the stars of heaven. The (famished) locust plunders (feasts) and flies away.

In the book "One Angel's Opinion," a man's hues are the visible manifestation of his invisible emotions, which Satán and his rebels (like locusts) feast on to receive their nourishment.

Hues are the entire visible color spectrum of light. It is light from which comes energy. Without God there is no light, and hence, no energy. Without energy there is no life.

In the book of John, Jesus came into the world as the Light of men, the giver of life.

Both the words "skin" and "light" in Hebrew are pronounced in English as "Or." (perhaps where the English word Aura originated?)

Jesus, like the lamb who covered Adam and Eve's sin in the Garden of Eden, gave his spotless "skin" to cover our sins AND was the "Light" of men.

After Noah emerges from the ark, God uses a rainbow of light arcing across a canopy-free sky to make a covenant with man to never again destroy the earth with a flood. The colors of the rainbow are a set of hues.

In the book of Revelation, John sees a rainbow behind the throne of God. A rainbow is made by separating the hues of light.

The color spectrum is made from waves of visible light. Some light waves; however, are invisible, such as gamma rays and radio waves. One might say Jesus is the visible spectrum of light, or "Jesus is the visible manifestation of an invisible God" where the triune God is the entire spectrum of both visible and invisible Light.

32. What are the frogs in the bottomless pit?

The concept comes from the following verse:

> Revelation 16:13 "And I saw three unclean spirits (full of lies/poisons), like frogs coming out of the mouth of the dragon, out of the mouth of the beast, and out of the mouth of the false prophet."

God uses that which is a biological fact to illustrate a spiritual reality: Evil men with unclean spirits are like poisonous frogs.

Dart frogs are poisonous frogs and are the most dangerous poisonous animals on earth.

> Poisons are lies that will spiritually kill anyone who ingests them (takes them into their thinking.)

"Due to their poison, the *Phyllobates* (dart) frogs taste vile to predators. Their *"Terribilis"* poison kills whatever eats it, with the exception of the snake *Liophis epinephelus*."
http://en.wikipedia.org/wiki/Golden_poison_frog

The snake *Liophis epinephelus* is resistant to the frog's poison, but is not completely immune.

> One Angel's Opinion sees this snake as Satán who does not seem to be affected by the poison produced but uses it for his production of poisonous darts to use against men, but he will eventually be destroyed by his own lies, therefore; he is not "entirely" immune.

(The poisonous) Frogs eat their skin during shedding, thus "recycling" any skin alkaloids (poisons).

> The spiritual application is that evil men "eat" ie: believe their own lies.

The chemical makeup of toxins in frogs varies from irritants to hallucinogens, convulsants, nerve poisons, and vasoconstrictors-

> Symbolic of the spiritual affect these poisonous lies have on societies, governments, and individuals.

These same frogs are not toxic at all when in captivity.

> God will take evil men into captivity who prescribe such lies, neutralizing their poison.

33. What is the basis for the broken compass Satán hands to his hierarchy?

God's truths are absolute, just like North on a compass.

Using a compass, a lost man is able to find his way home. A broken compass however, will keep a man walking in circles never knowing where he is or where he is going. The latter represents men who listen to lies (the broken compass) instead of beading on truth (North).

> Psalm 119:176 "I have gone astray like a lost sheep; Seek Your servant, For I do not forget Your commandments." NKJV

> Luke 9:25 "For what profit is it to a man if he gains the whole world, and is himself destroyed or lost?" NKJV

> Isaiah 53:6 "All we like sheep have gone astray; We have turned, every one, to his own way; And the LORD has laid on Him the iniquity of us all." NKJV

> Jeremiah 50:6 "My people have been lost sheep. Their shepherds have led them astray; They have turned them away on the mountains. They have gone from mountain to hill; They have forgotten their resting place." NKJV

34. Are there really an angel of fire and an angel of water?

> Rev 14:18 NKJV And another angel came out from the altar, who had power over fire, and he cried with a loud cry to him who had the sharp sickle, saying, "Thrust in your sharp sickle and gather the clusters of the vine of the earth, for her grapes are fully ripe."

Revelation 16:5-6 NIV
Then I heard the angel in charge of the waters say:

"You are just in these judgments, O Holy One, you who are and who were..."

35. Why did God destroy the earth and everything in it? Was it because of man's polluted DNA when fallen angels had relations with the daughters of men, or because mankind was violent?

Both have been inferred in scripture.

Genesis 6:2 NKJV
The sons of God saw the daughters of men, that they were beautiful; and they took wives for themselves of all whom they chose.

Genesis 6:4 NKJV
There were giants on the earth in those days, and also afterward, when the sons of God came in to the daughters of men and they bore children to them. Those were the mighty men who were of old, men of renown

Genesis 6:5-7 NKJV
Then the Lord saw that the wickedness of man was great in the earth; and that every intent of the thoughts of his heart was only evil continually. And the Lord was sorry that He had made man on the earth, and He was grieved in His heart.
So the Lord said, "I will destroy man whom I have created from the face of the earth; both man and beast, creeping thing and birds of the air, for I am sorry that I have made them."

Genesis 8:21 NKJV
And the Lord smelled a soothing aroma. Then the Lord said in His heart, "I will never again curse the ground for man's sake, although the imagination of man's heart is evil from his youth.

36. Was Naamah in Genesis 4:22 really the wife of Noah?

Not in scripture, but in Jewish tradition, yes.

37. Is there a "Mount of the Congregation" in scripture?

Yes, in Isaiah 14:13 (Note Lucifer is speaking from the perspective of being on earth.)

> "How you are fallen from heaven,
> O Lucifer, son of the morning!
> How you are cut down to the ground,
> You who weakened the nations!
>
> For you have said in your heart:
> 'I will ascend into heaven,

> I will exalt my throne above the stars of God;
> I will also sit <u>on the mount of the congregation
> On the farthest sides of the north</u>;
>
> I will ascend above the heights of the clouds,
> I will be like the Most High.'
>
> Yet you shall be brought down to Sheol,
> To the lowest depths of the Pit.

38. Did Lucifer walk among the "stones of fire" on the holy mountain of God?

> Yes, in Ezekiel 28:14 NASB
> "You were the anointed cherub who covers,
> And I placed you there.
> You were on the holy mountain of God;
> You walked in the midst of the stones of fire.

39. Where did the concept of capturing rebel angels and putting them in Hell come from?

> 2 Peter 2:4 NKJV
> For if God did not spare the angels who sinned, but cast them down to hell and delivered them into chains of darkness, to be reserved for judgment;

40. Where did the concept of "Lies" being like seedy, poisonous darts/ninja spikes/weapons originate?

> If there is fighting between God and the Fallen Angels, what do they use as weapons? Scripture says the Word of God (Truth) is like a two-edged sword. The opposite of Truth (the sword) is lies (seedy, fiery, poisonous darts.) The sword of Truth turns the darts of lies into useless weapons.
>
> > Ephesians 6:10-18 NKJV
> > Finally, my brethren, be strong in the Lord and in the power of His might. Put on the whole armor of God that you may be able to stand against the wiles of the devil; For we do not wrestle against flesh and blood, but against principalities, against powers, against the rulers of the darkness of this age, against spiritual hosts of wickedness in the heavenly places. Therefore take up the whole armor of God; that you may be

able to withstand in the evil day, and having done all, to stand.

Stand therefore, having girded your waist with truth, having put on the breastplate of righteousness, and having shod your feet with the preparation of the gospel of peace; above all, taking the shield of faith with which you will be able to quench all the fiery darts of the wicked one. And take the helmet of salvation, and the sword of the Spirit, which is the word of God; praying always with all prayer and supplication in the Spirit, being watchful to this end with all perseverance and supplication for all the saints—

Revelation 12:7 NKJV
And war broke out in heaven: Michael and his angels fought with the dragon; and the dragon and his angels fought, (What did they fight with? How are fallen angels conquered? I concluded it had to be with God's truth verses Satán's lies. If God's Truth is like a sword, then Satán's lies are the fiery darts/poisonous spikes.)

Psalm 140:3 NKJV
They sharpen their tongues like a serpent (Satán is referred to as a serpent/dragon/sea-serpent); the poison of asps is under their lips (lies). Selah

41. Is the book *One Angel's Opinion*, comparing Enoch with the rapture and Noah with the tribulation?

Yes. Just as Enoch was taken to heaven prior to the destruction of the earth in the tribulation of the flood, there are reasons to believe the future rapture will come just before the tribulation

42. What is the meaning in One Angel's Opinion, of God's pronouncement of One Hundred and Twenty years for men at the time of the flood? "My Spirit shall not strive with man forever. He is indeed flesh; yet his days shall be One Hundred and Twenty years."

The answer is threefold:

First: Man does not live beyond One Hundred and Twenty years if he is born after the flood.

Second: It took Noah One Hundred and Twenty years to build the ark.

Third: A Jewish jubilee is fifty years (every fifty years captives are released and land is returned to the original owner). In the six thousand years of man's history (according to the genealogies in the Bible) there have been One Hundred and Twenty jubilee periods of fifty years each. (120 times 50 = 6,000 years.) If man is at the end of his 6,000 years and the millennium is a thousand years totaling the predicted 7,000 years of man's time on earth, we may well be at the "end of the age" and waiting for the rapture of the saints.

43. Why is the spiritual world in the eleventh dimension? Why is man's rest in the thirteenth dimension?

The answer to this question is multi-faceted bringing into account scripture, Jewish tradition, and physics.

To review these concepts, in "One Angel's Opinion," the 11th dimension is the dimension of the invisible spirit world while the 13th dimension is the dimension in which God communicates with man through his dreams, thus 'uniting' with man.

THE 11th DIMENSION:

> Until recently, men have only been aware of the four dimensions of his reality through his perceptions of sight, touch, smell, feel, and smell. These four dimensions are length, height, width, and time. Scripture however, has always indicated a spirit world.
>
> Now, physics is also discovering more dimensions than the traditional four. There are dimensions unperceived and therefore invisible to the world of men.
>
> According to Physics, In order to unite the mathematical relationships of every force in the universe, there must be at least 11 or more dimensions in man's universe.
>
> This means taking the existing mathematical equations for all existing and known universal Forces to create one mathematical model that would incorporate all equations.
>
> This is referred to as "The Theory of Everything". It is also called "The String Theory." It is the holy grail in the world of mathematics; a model to explain the physics of the universe.
>
> > "In 1995, at the annual conference of string theorists at the University of Southern California (USC), Edward

Witten gave a speech on string theory that in essence **united** the five string theories that existed at the time, and giving birth to a new 11-dimensional theory called M-theory. M-theory was also foreshadowed in the work of Paul Townsend at approximately the same time. The flurry of activity that began at this time is sometimes called the second superstring revolution."

http://en.wikipedia.org/wiki/String_theory

THE 13TH DIMENSION:

When speaking of the number Thirteen (for the thirteenth dimension); consider this: it is the sum of seven and six. Seven is the number of God and six is the number of man. When united (through communication) they become the number thirteen. In "One Angel's Opinion" God communicates with man through his dreams in the thirteenth dimension. Throughout scripture God speaks to men in their dreams. This includes Abraham, Joseph, and Daniel in the Old Testament, and Joseph, the husband of Mary, in the New Testament.

According to Jewish tradition, thirteen is the holiest number because it refers to God being "One" based on Deuteronomy 6:4 (Where "One" refers to the word "Unity)

Deuteronomy 6:4 Hear, O Israel: The LORD (יְהוָה) (YHWH-Jehovah-Yehovah) our God (אֱלֹהֵינוּ) (Elohenu), is ONE (אֶחָד) (ehad).

Thirteen is the Jewish numerical value of the Hebrew word for ONE - (אֶחָד) "Ehad": (reading right to left) aleph (א), heth (ח), daleth (ד). Numerically, aleph is the number 1 + heth is the number 8 + deleth is the number 4 for a total of THIRTEEN.

Therefore, Ehad (the word for "One") = 13.

The meaning of the word "One" (which has a numerical value of 13) is "Unity."

The word One refers to the unity of God.

While many religions use Deuteronomy 6:4 to refute the trinity they overlook other verses that bring Deuteronomy 6:4

into a clear understanding of what the trinity is: The Father, the Son and the Spirit all working as ONE.

> Isaiah 9:6 NKJV
> For unto us a Child is born, Unto us **a Son** is given;
> And the government will be upon His shoulder.
> And His (the Son's) name will be called Wonderful, Counselor, **Mighty God, Everlasting Father**, Prince of Peace.

Since the Son is called both "Mighty God" in Isaiah 9:6, as well as "Everlasting Father," then Psalms 2:3 also refers to the fact that the Father and the Son (as well as the Holy Spirit) are tied together being ONE:

> Psalms 2:1-3 NKJV (The Determination of the Jewish Rulers to put Jesus to Death)
>
> Why do the (gentile ie: non-jewish) nations rage, And the (Jewish) people plot a vain thing? The (gentile) kings of the earth (Pilot and Herod) set themselves, And the (Jewish) rulers take counsel together, Against the Lord (God the Father) and against His Anointed (God the Son), saying,
> "Let us break Their (the Trinity's) bonds (Father, Son, Holy Spirit) in pieces
> And cast away Their (the Trinity's) cords (of authority) from us.

The Trinity is like an ATOM. The Atom is one Atom even if it has three electrons (Father, Son, Holy Spirit) spinning around the atom's nucleus of ONE character all in ONE accord. The Godhead, illustrated as an Atom, has an infinite amount of energy seen as Light. "In Him there is no darkness at all."

Since God is Light, and since some light waves are invisible and some light waves are visible (the color spectrum), then the Trinity can be compared to visible and invisible light waves. Jesus is the physical manifestation (the visible color spectrum of light waves) of an invisible God (the invisible light spectrum.)

So that Jesus, when speaking to Philip in John 14:9-10 said:

"Have I been with you so long, and yet you have not known Me, Philip? He who has seen Me has seen the Father; so how can you say, 'Show us the Father'? Do you not believe that I am in the Father, and the Father in Me?"

44. Zuben is called a "strong angel." Does scripture refer to some angels as being "strong?"

Revelation 5:2 NKJV
Then I saw a strong angel proclaiming with a loud voice, "Who is worthy to open the scroll and to loose its seals?"

2 Peter 2:10-11
They (false teachers) are not afraid to speak evil of dignitaries, whereas angels, who are greater in power and might, do not bring a reviling accusation against them before the Lord.

45. In Chapter One the angels fall down and worship God saying "Holy, holy, holy." What is your opinion on why they say holy three times?

Once for the Father, once for the Son, and once for the Holy Spirit.

46. What is the purpose for writing a book like this?

To encourage people to trust God, in spite of their questions.
God's ways are not our ways:

Isaiah 55:8 NKJV
"For My thoughts are not your thoughts, nor are your ways My ways," says the Lord.

Ezekiel 18:25 NKJV
"Yet you say, 'The way of the Lord is not fair.' Hear now, O house of Israel, is it not My way which is fair, and your ways which are not fair?

Ezekiel 18:29 NKJV
Yet the house of Israel says, 'The way of the Lord is not fair.' O house of Israel, is it not My ways which are fair, and your ways which are not fair?

Ultimately the hoped-for purpose in writing a book like this is to encourage people to read, re-read, and read again the pure source of all truth: God's Word-The Bible, and to come to a full understanding of his saving grace.

47. God made a Covenant, a pact, with man at the beginning of the book. Is there a scriptural reference for this?

Scripture calls Jesus the Lamb slain from BEFORE the foundation of the world. This means a decision, a pact, was made even before creation.

> Revelation 13:8
> All who dwell on the earth will worship him, whose names have not been written in the Book of Life of <u>the Lamb slain from the foundation of the world</u>.

There are similar scriptural events to shed light this is how God interacts with his creation. These are called "death covenants." They basically indicate a death sentence on the one making the covenant if he should break it.

The most notable is the covenant God made with Abraham.

> Genesis 15: 9-18
> So He said to him, "Bring Me a three-year-old heifer, a three-year-old female goat, a three-year-old ram, a turtledove, and a young pigeon." Then he brought all these to Him and cut them in two, down the middle, and placed each piece opposite the other; but he did not cut the birds in two. And when the vultures came down on the carcasses, Abram drove them away.
>
> Now when the sun was going down, a deep sleep fell upon Abram; and behold, horror and great darkness fell upon him. Then He said to Abram: "Know certainly that your descendants will be strangers in a land that is not theirs, and will serve them, and they will afflict them four hundred years. And also the nation whom they serve I will judge; afterward they shall come out with great possessions. Now as for you, you shall go to your fathers in peace; you shall be buried at a good old age. But in the fourth generation they shall return here, for the iniquity of the Amorites is not yet complete."
>
> And it came to pass, when the sun went down and it was dark, that behold, there appeared a smoking oven and a burning torch that <u>passed between those pieces</u>. On the same day the Lord made a covenant with Abram.

48. Abel's name means "whiff or breeze," doesn't it also mean "unnecessary?"

> Yes, Abel seems to lack substance.
>
> In Strong's concordance his name is Havel, or Abel: H1893, H1892.
>
> The definition of his name is "Nothingness, Un-needed or not necessary."
>
> Throughout the story the reader will find Adam telling his son "that isn't necessary," thus negating him.
>
> If Adam and Eve believed their redeemer was in Cain's birthright, then why would Abel be necessary?
>
> When Cain killed Abel, in death, Abel became "Nothingness."
>
> Abel reminds us that our days are like a breeze, like nothingness:
>
>> Psalm 103:15-19
>> As for man, his days are like grass; as a flower of the field, so he flourishes. For the wind passes over it, and it is gone, And its place remembers it no more.
>>
>> But the mercy of the Lord is from everlasting to everlasting on those who fear Him, and His righteousness to children's children, to such as keep His covenant, And to those who remember His commandments to do them.
>>
>> The Lord has established His throne in heaven, and His kingdom rules over all.

49. The Title indicates "One Angel's Opinion, Auroran's Declaration" is Volume One. Are there more volumes to come? Is this the beginning of a series?

> Yes. There might be a total of six volumes, three more are almost completed.
>
> Watch for them at:
> http://bgro44.wix.com/bgwriting